Yang the Third and Her Impossible Family

Lensey Namioka

Illustrated by Kees de Kiefte

A Yearling Book

For Rita
L. N.

For Enny
K. de K.

Published by
Bantam Doubleday Dell Books for Young Readers
a division of
Bantam Doubleday Dell Publishing Group, Inc.
1540 Broadway
New York, New York 10036

ISBN: 0-440-41231-5

Reprinted by arrangement with Little, Brown & Company
Printed in the United States of America

August 1996

10 9 8 7 6 5 4 3 2 1

CWO

1

The Conners are inviting us for Thanksgiving dinner!" yelled Fourth Brother as he hung up the phone.

The Conners are our neighbors here in Seattle, and Matthew Conner is Fourth Brother's best friend. He takes violin lessons from Father, and he also plays in our family string quartet.

Eldest Brother plays first violin, and Second Sister plays viola. I'm the third sister in the Yang family, and I play cello. Fourth Brother plays baseball. He has a terrible ear, and he was relieved when Matthew took his place as the second violin.

We were all happy about the invitation. For weeks, we had been hearing about the American holiday called Thanksgiving. Since coming to this country, we have tried our best to do everything properly, but when Mother heard that preparing a Thanksgiving dinner involved roasting a turkey, she was horrified.

"I can't even roast a pigeon," she cried. "If I tried to wrestle with a turkey, I'd lose!"

We didn't have an oven in China. Almost nobody does. If you want a roast duck or chicken, you buy it already cooked in the store — sometimes chopped into bite-size pieces. When Mother saw the big box under the stove in our Seattle kitchen, she didn't know what it was at first. Even now, months later, she was still nervous about the black cavity and thought of it as a chamber of horrors.

Now we'd learn how real Americans celebrate Thanksgiving. We'd get a delicious meal, like the ones I had seen illustrated in all the papers and magazines.

What excited me most was hearing that Holly Hanson and her mother were invited, too. Holly was in the school orchestra with me. She played in the viola section, so I didn't get a chance to talk to her much. But I really wanted to.

When I was little, we had a tin candy box, and on the lid was the picture of a princess with curly blond hair. Holly Hanson looked just like the princess in that picture. She was in a couple of my classes in school, and she always spoke in a soft, unhurried way. I thought that if the princess on the candy box spoke, she would sound just like that.

At the Conners' I would finally get a chance to get acquainted with Holly. But I was nervous, too, because I wanted so much to have my family make a good impression.

When Thanksgiving Day came, the whole Yang family showed up at the Conners' exactly at two o'clock. We'd thought two was a strange time for a dinner party, but Matthew explained that since people stuff themselves at Thanksgiving, eating early gives everybody a chance to digest.

We all tried to look our best for the dinner. Father had on the dark suit he wore for playing in public. Instead of her usual cotton slacks and shirt, Mother wore a dress she had bought at the Goodwill store for three dollars. It was a very nice dress, but on her slender figure, the huge shoulder pads made her look like a stranger — an aggressive stranger.

Eldest Brother wore a suit, too. Second Sister and I wore skirts, and Fourth Brother had on his clean blue jeans. I hoped we'd all look presentable when we met Holly and her mother.

Mrs. Hanson and Holly arrived a few minutes after we did, and we were introduced. My parents had told us we should all shake hands with the Hansons. Mrs. Hanson looked a little startled when six Yang hands were extended toward her. Although our etiquette book clearly said shaking hands is the polite thing to do, I decided that in America, children don't usually do it.

Except for that, things seemed to be going pretty well. The dining table looked beautiful, with china plates and tall wine glasses — even for the young people, who drank juice. I carefully studied the way the knives, forks, and spoons were set.

I was delighted when Mrs. Conner seated me next to Holly, but the only thing I could think to say was "I've seen you in the orchestra."

It sounded stupid as soon as I'd said it, but Holly just nodded and murmured something.

The dinner began with Mr. Conner saying some words of thanks for his family's good fortune. It was like a toast at a Chinese banquet, and I thought he sounded very dignified.

Mrs. Conner carried the whole roast turkey into the dining room on a platter, and we all exclaimed at the size of the turkey. It was the largest bird I had ever seen, dead or alive.

Mr. Conner began sharpening a wicked-looking knife. Then he took up the knife and a big fork, and began to cut thin slices of meat from the bird.

We Yangs looked at one another in wonder. Instead of complaining about being made to do the slicing, Mr. Conner looked pleased and proud.

After slicing a pile of turkey meat, Mr. Conner started to scoop from the stomach of the bird. I was horrified. Had Mrs. Conner forgotten to dress the turkey and left all the guts behind?

Chicken is an expensive treat in China. When Mother wanted to boil or stir-fry a chicken, she had to buy the bird live to make sure it was fresh. Killing, plucking, and dressing the chicken was a gruesome job, and Mother hated it. The worst part was pulling all the guts out of the stomach. Sometimes, when the bird was a hen, she would even find a cluster of eggs inside.

Watching Mr. Conner scooping away, I was embarrassed for him. I exchanged glances with the rest of my family, and I could see that they were dismayed, too.

To my astonishment — and relief — what

Mr. Conner scooped out was not the messy intestines. Mrs. Conner had not forgotten to dress the bird after all. She had stuffed the stomach of the bird with a savory mixture of bread and onions!

We gasped with admiration, and Mrs. Conner looked pleased. "I hope you like the stuffing. I'm trying out a new recipe."

Mr. Conner placed some slices of turkey meat on each plate, then added a spoonful of the stuffing mixture. Next he ladled a brown sauce over everything. He passed the first plate to Mother.

"Oh, I couldn't take this," Mother said politely. She passed the plate on to Mrs. Hanson.

Mrs. Hanson was jammed up against Mother's shoulder pad at the crowded table. She passed the plate back to Mother. "Oh, no, it's meant for you, Mrs. Yang."

Mother handed the plate back again. "You're so much older, Mrs. Hanson, so you should be served first."

Mrs. Hanson froze. In the silence, I could hear the sauce going *drip, drip* from Mr. Conner's ladle.

"What makes you think so?" asked Mrs. Hanson stiffly. "Just what makes you think I'm older?"

"Mom, let's skip it," Holly whispered.

I had already learned that in America it isn't considered an honor to be old. Instead of respecting older people, as we do, Americans think it is pitiful to be old. Mrs. Hanson must have thought that Mother was trying to insult her. Would Mother say something else embarrassing?

She didn't disappoint me. "Well, how old are you, then?" Mother asked Mrs. Hanson.

I winced. In school, I had once asked a friend how old our teacher was. We do this a lot. When we meet a stranger, we often ask him how old he is. My friend told me, however, that in America it's rude to ask people's ages. I was really grateful to her for the warning.

After Mother's question, Mrs. Hanson sat completely still. "I am thirty-six," she replied finally, each syllable falling like a chunk of ice.

"Oh, really?" said Mother brightly. "You look much older!"

A whuffling sound came from Matthew and his brother, Eric. Unable to look at the Hansons,

I stole a glance at Mr. Conner. His face was bright red, and he seemed to be having trouble breathing. Mrs. Conner was bent over, as if in pain. I looked down at my plate and wished I could disappear.

Somehow, the dinner went on. Mrs. Hanson finally unclenched her jaw and told Mrs. Conner how delicious the cranberry sauce was. I figured she was referring to the red sticky mound of poisonous-looking berries. I put a berry in my mouth and almost gagged at its sour taste. Next to me, Fourth Brother quietly spat his cranberries into his paper napkin. When he caught my eye, he looked guilty. He wadded up the napkin and stuffed it into his pocket. I hoped he wouldn't forget about it later.

The rest of the food was delicious, though. I thought the stuffing tasted even better than the turkey meat. The good food seemed to relax everybody, and people began to chat. Eldest Brother, who liked to do carpentry, was asking Mr. Conner's advice about various kinds of saws. Mrs. Hanson and Mrs. Conner talked about what kind of cake they were planning to make for the bake sale at the next PTA meeting.

I took a deep breath and turned to Holly.

"How do you like the piece we're playing for the winter concert? The violas have a pretty good part."

Holly picked at her cranberries. "I may have to pass up the concert. My viola teacher wants me to play in a recital, and I have to spend all my time practicing for that."

Holly spoke in her usual pleasant voice, but she didn't sound enthusiastic about the recital.

"Do you like your viola teacher?" I asked. "My father teaches viola, as well as violin, you know."

Mrs. Hanson turned her head. "Holly takes lessons from the first violist of the Seattle Symphony!"

I flushed. She sounded as if she thought I was drumming up lessons for my father.

Father looked interested. "Does Holly take lessons from Silverman? He's a marvelous musician! It must be wonderful to be accepted as his pupil!"

Mrs. Hanson's expression softened. "Holly works awfully hard. She can be a regular whirlwind at times!"

I stopped worrying. Apparently Mrs. Hanson had got over her anger at being called old, and we Yangs were not disgracing ourselves. We all used our knives and forks correctly and waited for permission before helping ourselves from the serving dishes in the middle of the table.

I asked Holly about herself. "Do you have any brothers or sisters?"

"No, there's just Mom and me at home." She added softly, "My parents were divorced three years ago."

I tried to find something sympathetic to say but couldn't think of anything. Holly's expression didn't tell me much. "Do you spend much time with your father?" I finally asked.

"I stay with him during the summer," said Holly. "He has a boat and takes me sailing."

I was impressed. "A boat? Your father must be rich!"

As soon as the words left my mouth, I wished I could take them back. I had forgotten that in America it isn't polite to discuss money. However hard I tried, I just couldn't remember everything.

Holly was silent for a moment. Finally she said, "My mom supports the two of us. She works in the records department in a hospital. But Dad pays for my music lessons." She looked curiously at me. "Does your mother work?"

"No, she spends all her time shopping and

cooking," I admitted. Suddenly my mother, with her ridiculous shoulder pads, looked dumpy sitting next to the elegant Mrs. Hanson, who worked with records in a hospital. Were they LP records, cassette tapes, or CDs? I wondered. It sounded like a glamorous job.

"I wish my mother had a job," I said wistfully. Mother had been a professional pianist, but in Seattle she hadn't been able to find work.

At least Second Sister and I earned some money baby-sitting, which is something girls don't do in China. If Chinese parents have to go out, they usually try to get the grandparents to look after the children.

"Do you do any baby-sitting?" I asked.

"I do a little," said Holly. Suddenly she smiled. "What I like best is to baby-sit dogs."

"Baby-sit dogs," I repeated slowly. "You mean dog-sit?"

Holly laughed. I could see *this* was something she really enjoyed talking about. "When my neighbors are busy, I take their dogs for walks," she explained. "I just love animals."

"If Holly had her way, our house would be overflowing with pets," said Mrs. Hanson.

"Did you keep pets in China?" Holly asked me.

I shook my head. "We didn't have room."

"We could barely squeeze our family into our Shanghai apartment," said Father, "much less have room for pets."

"Until recently, it was actually illegal to keep a dog in many cities," added Mother. "If a dog was heard barking, the police would come to investigate."

Holly looked shocked. "How about cats, then? Are you allowed to keep cats?"

"Cats are allowed," said Father. "They don't take up much room, and they don't create a sanitation problem in the streets. But keeping them is still a luxury most people can't afford."

"Well, it's different here," said Mrs. Hanson. "Holly and I have a cat and six kittens at the moment."

"If you have a house with a yard, you'd have room enough for a cat," Holly said to me. "Do you live in a house?"

I wondered why she sounded so eager as she asked the question. Before I could say anything, Father answered. "We're renting half of a house, but it would be quite impossible for us to keep a cat. We have so many instruments and piles of sheet music lying around that any kind of pet would be a disaster."

The excitement faded from Holly's face, and I knew our family had disappointed her in some way. I wondered why.

Mrs. Conner began to clear the dinner plates. Matthew and his brother, Eric, jumped up to help her. Fourth Brother also got up, but Mrs. Conner told him to sit down again. "Two helpers are all I need, Sprout. The kitchen isn't big enough for more than that."

"Sprout?" said Father. I knew he loved stir-fried bean sprouts. He looked eagerly around the table and was disappointed when he didn't see any.

I laughed. "Sprout is what everybody calls Fourth Brother, Father."

My American friends call me Mary, the name I picked for myself, since my Chinese name, Yingmei, is too hard for them to remember. In fact I had trouble remembering *American* names when I first came. I still keep a list of new words and phrases for memorizing, and a lot of the entries are names.

My family could never remember my new American name, though. When people mentioned Mary, the Yangs would say, "Who is Mary?" So it was good to see Father puzzled by Sprout for a change.

Mr. Conner nodded. "Yeah, Sprout is a good name for the little guy." He added quickly, "The little guy with the big bat." Mr. Conner was proud of Fourth Brother's success with baseball, because he was the one who had coached him.

Mr. Conner was right. Sprouts look small and weedy, but they push up from the earth with a lot of determination. Fourth Brother is like that.

After the plates were cleared, Mrs. Conner brought in dessert: ice cream and three different kinds of pies. From the way their eyes were shining, I guessed that Eric and Matthew thought this was the best part of the meal. Personally, I enjoyed the turkey and the stuffing so much that I didn't feel like eating anything more, especially something sweet.

Again, the first slice of pie went to Mother. This time she didn't try to pass it to Mrs. Hanson. She had learned her lesson.

Mrs. Hanson looked at the piece of pie served to her. "Oh, I couldn't eat all this. I've already put on two pounds this month, and I can't afford to gain another ounce."

"Of course you can afford it!" Mrs. Conner said heartily. "You're so skinny, you could put on ten pounds and still look terrific."

Mother was staring at Mrs. Hanson and Mrs. Conner during this exchange. We Chinese think that being fat is good. It's a sign of good fortune. Thin people are considered unfortunate and miserable.

But I knew that here, being thin is supposed to be attractive. A lot of the girls in school are worried about their weight, and some of them even go on diets.

I saw Mother open her mouth. Don't say it, Mother, I wanted to shout. Don't say it!

But she did. Radiating good will, Mother said, "Why, you're not skinny at all, Mrs. Hanson. You're actually quite fat!"

List of AMERICAN WORDS by Mary

2

We had been living in America for almost a year, and I had finally learned the names of all the American holidays. But ever since that dinner with the Conners, I'll always think of Thanksgiving Day as Memorial Day, because I'll remember it for a long, long time. So will Mrs. Hanson.

As soon as we got home from the dinner, I called up Holly and tried to explain. "With us Chinese, it's good to be old and fat. My mother was just paying your mother compliments."

"That's what I guessed," said Holly. "Mom and I talked it over, and after she calmed down a bit, she admitted your mother probably didn't mean to insult her."

Although that Thanksgiving dinner was one of the most embarrassing, it wasn't the first time in America that my family had given me some bad moments.

Even Fourth Brother could be awfully trying. He's a good baseball player, and when his team won lots of games last season, people told me what a great kid he was. Still, he managed to do a few things that made people laugh at him.

For instance: I always make sandwiches for the two of us in the morning, and at first I just used leftover food I found in the refrigerator. We usually have stir-fried bean sprouts, because that's what Father likes and Mother prepares a big dish of it almost every meal.

When I found out that almost all my classmates brought sandwiches made with peanut butter and jelly, I talked Mother into buying some. She didn't want to at first. Jams and jellies are expensive in China, and peanut butter is something rare you find in stores for foreign tourists.

But Mother changed her mind when she found out how cheap and easy it was to buy peanut butter and jelly in Seattle. We got grape jelly, because I had counted more grape jelly than any other kind at my lunch table in school.

The next morning, I made us the kind of sandwiches that were just like everybody else's.

But after school, Fourth Brother told me he hadn't liked his.

"Why?" I asked him. "Is it the grape jelly? I can ask Mother to get some other flavor."

Fourth Brother shuffled his feet. "I hate peanut butter!" he said finally.

"I thought you liked peanuts! You're always eating peanuts, and the shells used to get into your violin. Remember how they rattled?"

Fourth Brother laughed. Then he shook his head. "I love peanuts, but peanut butter sticks to the roof of my mouth and gums up my lips. Today my teacher complained that I mumbled."

After that Fourth Brother went back to eating bean sprout sandwiches, and, since many of his friends had trouble remembering his name, Yingtao, they just started calling him "Sprout."

Fourth Brother didn't realize that in America, kids are supposed to hate vegetables. So when he ate all those bean sprouts, the other kids probably thought he was weird. I was terribly embarrassed for him, until I realized that he didn't mind being called Sprout. Still, I didn't like being known as "Sprout's sister." What did that make me — a soy bean?

Fourth Brother and I had always been close.

We're the youngest in our family, and I've felt protective toward him. He's small for his age — even for a Chinese boy — and I love the way he grits his teeth when he's really determined. The two of us had been a team, and we'd managed to get through some hard times together.

But Fourth Brother didn't seem to need my help anymore. He might eat sprouts, but he was popular in school because he was a good athlete. When we first moved to Seattle, he was kind of forlorn in school, and I would eat lunch with him to keep him company. But now he had his own friends.

I felt wistful when I looked at Fourth Brother and his friend Matthew having such a good time together. I didn't have trouble *meeting* the kids

in my class, but it was hard to get close to them. It seemed like everyone at my school had a best friend. If only Holly and I could become best friends, like Fourth Brother and Matthew. Then we could do everything together.

Although Mrs. Hanson wasn't mad at my mother anymore, I still got nowhere in becoming friends with Holly. Orchestra would be where I'd have my best chance of getting together with her, I thought. After rehearsal, the players in my section sometimes chatted about the music as we put our instruments away.

But by the time I finished wrestling my cello into its canvas bag, Holly would be gone. She always hurried off right after rehearsal.

During recess, I'd look at Holly surrounded by her circle of friends. One day, when they stood around looking bored, I tried to think how I could join the group. Finally I gathered up my courage and walked over to them. "Would you like to play a Chinese game?" I said brightly. "It's called Open and Secret Seven. We form a circle and —"

"No, thanks," interrupted Debbie, one of the girls. "If we want to play games, we've got some of our own."

After that, it took a thicker skin than mine

to force myself into their group. (I had been
puzzled at first by the phrase "thick skin." I
thought it meant a callus!)

A few days later, something happened that
gave me my chance. We usually play outside
during recess, even when it drizzles — and in
a Seattle winter it drizzles a lot. That day, it was
really pouring. Our elementary school has a cov-
ered basketball court, and we usually huddle
there when the weather is bad.

Suddenly I overheard Holly's voice. She and
her friends were leaning against the cyclone
fence on one side of the court. "Our cat had six

kittens in her litter," she said. "We named them Errol Flynn, Greta Garbo, Clark Gable, Marilyn Monroe, Cary Grant, and Rita Hayworth."

"Hey, cool," said Jill, one of the other girls. "You named them all after old movie stars!"

"It was my idea," said Holly, "because Mom and I like to watch videos of old movies."

In China, we might name an animal Little Flower, Star, or something like that. But we'd never give it a human name, the way Americans sometimes do.

Our neighbors, the Sylvesters, used to have a dog named Denny. Or maybe Denny is Mr. Sylvester's name, and the dog was Benny. Since Mr. Sylvester doesn't always wear his false teeth, it's hard to understand him sometimes. Mrs. Sylvester has a soft voice and mumbles, so I have a hard time understanding her, too. Her name is Jenny — or maybe Jenny was the dog's name. I'm always getting mixed up!

"Are you going to keep any of the kittens?" one of the girls asked Holly.

Holly shook her head. "I have to find homes for all of them. So far I've found homes for all except Rita. Mom says unless I find someone to take her soon, she'll take her to the pound.

And you know what happens to kittens in a pound."

Kittens in a pound? Maybe she had said "pond." In China people sometimes drown unwanted kittens. Maybe they did that here, too.

"You're sure you can't take her, Kim?" Holly asked. She sounded desperate.

The girl called Kim shook her head. "Gee, I'm sorry, Holly. But my brother, Jason, is allergic to cats."

I glanced over at Holly's group. Kim was the one I saw most often with Holly. At first I thought they must be best friends, but then I noticed that Kim acted more like an attendant to the princess rather than a fellow princess.

No, come to think of it, Kim was more like a court jester. She has bright eyes, and she likes to roll them around when she says something funny. Now, when she had to refuse Holly, her eyes were still and downcast.

The rest of the girls also looked regretful. They murmured things like, "I've got one kitten already, and that's all my mom would let me take," or, "Sorry, Holly. You know I'd help if I could."

Before I realized it, I found myself on my

feet, walking over to Holly. "Did you say you want to give away a kitten? I'll take it."

Holly didn't seem to believe me at first. I didn't believe me, myself, when I remembered what Father had said about our instruments and piles of music.

Finally Holly smiled. "You're a good sport, Mary. But are you sure you want to do it?"

"I'm sure," I said firmly. "I love cats."

Holly heaved a big sigh of relief. "That's wonderful! Can you come over after school today to look at the kitten?"

"All right," I said, and waved good-bye to Holly and her friends. I had actually been invited to Holly's house!

As I left the group, I heard Debbie's whisper. "Chinese people eat dogs. Maybe they eat cats, too. Maybe Mary loves cats the way she loves ice cream."

There were giggles from a couple of the others, and I saw that Kim's eyes were rolling around again. My face was red, but I managed to walk away with dignity.

After school, Fourth Brother and I went home together. I wasn't sure how much to tell him. He'd probably think I was crazy to offer to take the kitten. The more I thought about it, I started to think I was crazy, too.

It just wouldn't be safe to keep a pet in our house. As Father had said at Thanksgiving, our living and dining rooms are filled with piles of sheet music and instruments. We practically breathe, eat, and drink music. Even when we aren't playing, we leave our instruments around, because we might pick them up at any moment to play some passages.

We all have to take good care of our instruments. Our parents do without furniture or curtains in order to buy the best instruments they can afford. A kitten could do a lot of damage. A drop of sweat slid down my nose at the thought of claws scratching my cello — or worse, Father's violin.

I began to wish desperately that I could take back my offer. Then I remembered Holly's delight and relief. I remembered Kim's eyes rolling around and the laughing faces of the others. No, I simply had to stand by my offer.

"Is something wrong, Third Sister?" Fourth Brother asked me. We understand each other better than the rest of the family, and he can usually tell when I'm in trouble.

I looked at him. He sometimes has good

ideas. Maybe he could help. I took a deep breath. "What do you think of the idea of getting a kitten?"

He blinked. "*Us?* A kitten for *our* family?"

"Yes, a kitten all our own! We would play with it and feed it and take care of it. Wouldn't it be fun?"

A big smile broke over his face. "That's true! We live in a house now, not an apartment!"

Then Fourth Brother's smile faded. He began to see some of the difficulties. "Would Father and Mother agree?"

"We don't have to tell them immediately," I said quickly.

There was a silence.

"I'm going to Holly Hanson's house this afternoon," I continued. "She's got an extra kitten that we can have. Want to come? If I decide to take it home with me, I might need your help."

Fourth Brother stared at me. We had done some pretty wild things together, but now he looked uneasy.

"Well?" I asked him. "Are you coming with me or not?"

This time he was the one who had to swallow hard. "All right. I'll come with you."

3

She was just a scrap of fur on legs — tottering legs.

"She's the runt of the litter," said Holly, picking up the kitten.

I didn't know what a runt was, but I was too embarrassed to admit it. Fourth Brother wasn't too embarrassed, though. "What does 'runt' mean?" he asked.

"It means she's the smallest and the weakest," said Holly. It was true. There were several kittens crowding around the mother cat, trying to reach her nipples. The smallest kitten, the runt, couldn't push her way into the warm circle and was left outside. It mewed pitifully, and its voice sounded like the squeak of a door — a tiny, tiny door.

"Sounds like my violin squeaking," said Fourth Brother, laughing at the kitten, who tried to walk but fell over.

My insides melted at the helpless little thing. *Runt*, that's a good word: I would have to write it down on my list of new English words.

There was something about this runt that went straight to my heart. The kitten and I were alike — trying to squeeze in where we weren't wanted.

I picked her up gently and held her to my cheek. I could feel her tiny heart beating, and after a moment, a soft rumble started. She was purring! I found myself crooning nonsense to her in Chinese.

"I guess you like her," said Holly, smiling. "She's Rita, named after Rita Hayworth."

I remembered Holly saying that all the kittens were named after old movie stars. I had never heard of Rita Hayworth, but I liked the sound of her name.

"Are you planning to take her with you today?" asked Holly. "Some of the other owners are picking up their kittens later."

Now that I was holding Rita's fluffy little body in my hands, I found it very hard to put her

down. "I'd like to take her home with me," I said softly.

Holly began to give me instructions on how to care for the kitten. "We didn't want to give any of our kittens away until they've learned from their mother to bury their poop. If you give them away right after they're born, they never learn."

I was impressed. "How come you know so much about animals?"

"I always wanted to be a vet — you know, an animal doctor," she said. "So I've read lots of books about how to take care of pets."

"But I thought you were going to be a musician," I said, remembering how proud Mrs. Hanson had been when she'd said Holly was taking lessons from the first violist of the Seattle Symphony.

Holly shook her head and looked away. "My parents are the ones who want me to take music lessons."

Fourth Brother wanted to hold the kitten, too, but when I tried to hand her to him, she dug her claws into my shirt and wouldn't let go. Her claws weren't long enough to hurt. I laughed.

"Are you going to keep her in your room?"

asked Holly. "The weather's too cold for her to stay outside."

Fourth Brother and I looked at each other. On the way over, we had already decided where we were going to hide the kitten. "We'll keep her inside, where it's warm," I said carefully.

What we had planned was to keep her in the basement of the house we were renting. The basement was large, and it was cluttered with things left behind by the landlord and some of the previous renters. There were all sorts of dark corners where we could hide the kitten.

"Do you have a litter box?" Holly asked next.

"Litter box?" I stared at her, startled by this sudden change of subject. All I knew was that in America you can get fined for littering.

Holly sighed. "I guess I'd better explain. A litter box is where the kitten can go to the bathroom."

Again I was startled. Rita using the bathroom? Didn't cats lick themselves clean? Then I remembered that when American kids say they have to go to the bathroom, they mean something different.

"You have to be careful about leaving piles of paper or other stuff around," continued Holly. "Once Cary Grant pooped on a sweater

Mom was knitting. Boy, was she mad! We washed and washed, but couldn't get rid of the smell, and we finally had to throw it away."

I had already guessed what "pooped" meant. What Holly said about piles of paper worried me. "How about our sheet music?"

"Never let her get near your sheet music!" warned Holly. "Marilyn Monroe tore up my homework the other day. I guess she was trying to sharpen her claws. Rita Hayworth has very sharp claws, too."

Oh, no! How could I keep the kitten away from our music? As for the litter box, maybe I could dig up some garden dirt and put it in a box. But I'd have to do it out of sight of the Sylvesters.

The Sylvesters' dog, Benny, used to sit blinking in the yard when it was sunny. I was scared of it at first, because the only dogs I had seen in China were fierce watchdogs in the countryside. But I soon discovered that Denny was too old to attack anybody. It had died a couple of months ago. Mrs. Sylvester was awfully sad, but I was glad Jenny wasn't around any more. It would have sniffed out the kitten.

"Here, why don't I write down a list of instructions for taking care of the kitten?" said

Holly. She sounded like the nurse in our local clinic.

While Holly was writing her list, I whispered to Fourth Brother in Chinese, "We'd better not let the rest of the family know about Rita for a while. We'll have to smuggle her home."

I didn't have to say more. He knew what I meant. "How can we do that?" he asked.

I thought of an idea. "How about carrying her in your violin case? Can you go get it?"

He opened his mouth to protest. Fourth Brother hates the violin, but that didn't mean he liked the idea of cat hairs in the case.

"You can line it with my pajamas," I said quickly.

He wasn't happy, but he agreed to go. He got back just as Mrs. Hanson came home.

She stared when she saw me opening the violin case and lifting Rita into it. "What on earth are you doing?" she cried.

I was so startled that I nearly dropped the case. Rita jumped out and scampered under the kitchen table.

"We're — uh — planning to carry the kitten back home," I explained lamely. "It seems like a nice safe place to put her."

Mrs. Hanson stared. "That kitten needs air! It will suffocate inside that case!"

"Why don't you just carry her in a cardboard box?" asked Holly. She went to the coat closet and took out a large carton. "You can use this."

Fourth Brother and I looked at the box. Then we looked at each other. "She might be able to jump out," I said finally. "The violin case is better. I won't close it completely. See, I'll leave it open a bit."

It was a weak argument, and I could see that neither Mrs. Hanson nor Holly was convinced. Suddenly Mrs. Hanson's eyes narrowed. "Are you trying to hide the kitten from your parents? You haven't told them about it yet!"

There was no use denying it. "No, I haven't told them," I admitted in a small voice.

"In other words, you know they wouldn't approve," said Mrs. Hanson. She shook her head. "I'm sorry, Mary, but I can't let you take the kitten."

I tried to swallow the lump in my throat. "What — what will happen to the kitten, then?"

Mrs. Hanson's face looked stern. "It will just have to go to the pound."

Or did she mean pond? Was she really planning to drown the kitten? Rita played happily under the kitchen table, unaware of her fate.

Holly looked stricken. "Oh, Mom, not the pound! Mary can talk her parents around!"

"We can do it!" declared Fourth Brother. The others stared at him in surprise. He continued confidently. "We've done harder things than that! We even managed to persuade my parents to let me stop taking violin lessons!"

"Please let us try, Mrs. Hanson," I pleaded. "If it really doesn't work, then you can take the kitten to the pond."

Under the table, Rita was chasing her own tail, thinking it was a mouse, maybe. She looked so adorable that my throat tightened at the thought of losing her.

"Mom, I'm sure Mary can get her parents to agree," pleaded Holly.

Finally Mrs. Hanson's face softened. "Oh, all right, but only if Mary promises to tell her parents about the kitten."

I nodded eagerly. "I promise!" What I didn't say was *when* I would tell them.

As we went to the door, I asked Holly if she would like to come with us. "You can help us settle Rita down in her new home," I suggested.

"We're planning to keep her in our basement until we tell my parents."

"All right," said Holly. "Then I can check if your basement is warm and well ventilated."

Holly was finally visiting my house! It marked another step in becoming friends with her.

Fourth Brother carried the violin case in his arms as we walked home. It kept tilting back and forth like a seesaw as Rita moved around inside. I was afraid he might drop it, and I wanted to take it from him. But I knew it would look funny if I carried his violin case for him.

We sighed with relief when we finally made it home. "Safe at last!" I said.

I had spoken too soon. Before we could head for the basement, Second Sister came to the door. When I saw how she looked, I was sorry after all that Holly had come over.

Second Sister was in her "I'm Chinese and I don't care who knows it" mood. She was wearing her blue cotton jacket with the high collar, and on her feet were the black cloth shoes she had brought from China. There was a hole in the right one, and her big toe stuck out.

When Holly saw me staring at Second Sister's feet, she looked down, too. I saw her lips twitch.

If only Holly hadn't already met Second Sister

at the Thanksgiving dinner! I wanted so much to tell her that we had come to the wrong house and that this Chinese girl with the funny pigtails was a perfect stranger.

Second Sister didn't give me a chance. She stared at the violin case in Fourth Brother's hands. "When did you start playing the violin again?" She tried to look glad, but she couldn't quite hide the dismay from her voice.

The violin case jumped in Fourth Brother's hands, and he grabbed at it quickly before it dropped. "Uh . . . You all looked so happy making music," he mumbled, "that I decided to give the violin another try."

Second Sister swallowed. "Well, that's wonderful!" she managed to say. "Wait till I tell everybody. They'll be delighted!"

A squeak came from the violin case. To cover the noise, I began to hum loudly. "That's the piece we're practicing in our orchestra," I said.

Holly tried to help me by humming a few bars, too, but she was a little out of tune. "Yes, it's a lovely piece," she said.

"I'd better do some practicing right away," said Fourth Brother. "I have a lot of catching up to do."

Second Sister winced. I said quickly, "Yes,

Fourth Brother has to work hard. We'll go down to the basement, where it's nice and quiet — and far from everybody."

"Yes, do that," said Second Sister, relieved.

Her relief was nothing compared to ours. When we reached the basement, Fourth Brother set the seesawing case down and rubbed his arms. "I was getting a cramp from holding on so tightly," he complained.

I opened the case, squatted down, and looked at Rita, who stretched and yawned, opening her tiny pink jaw. Again, I felt my insides melt. I held out a finger, and she promptly began chewing on it. I giggled when I felt her little teeth trying to bite down. It didn't hurt, only tickled.

"I think she's hungry," said Holly. "You'll have to get her something to eat right away."

"I'll get some milk," said Fourth Brother, going back upstairs.

"I think a cardboard box is just the right thing for Rita's home," said Holly. "It would help keep her warm." She looked around the dark basement. "It's rather cold down here, isn't it?"

I immediately felt guilty. "Of course Rita won't live here permanently!"

I finally found a carton half filled with kindling. I dumped the wood out and brought the box over. Rita was gone. I felt a moment of panic. Had she raced upstairs and let Second Sister catch sight of her?

But then Holly laughed. "There she is!"

I saw that my pajamas were heaving, and I found Rita tangled up under them. I laughed, too, and rescued her from the tangle. But I stopped laughing when I caught a whiff of the pajamas.

"You'll have to buy some kitty litter as soon as possible," said Holly, wrinkling her nose. "Then she can go to the bathroom in it and not use your pajamas."

I had a sinking feeling. Whatever kitty litter was, buying it would cost money. I took away my dirty pajamas and looked for something else to line Rita's box with. There was a brown paper bag on the ground, and I opened it to see whether it was empty. Like a streak of lightning, Rita rushed into the bag and rustled around furiously inside. Then she backed out of the bag and looked up at me, as if to say, "Wow, that was fun!"

Suddenly I remembered the time in school when I'd wanted to teach the girls in Holly's group a Chinese game and they hadn't been interested. Now I realized I should have done what Rita was doing. When there was nobody to play with, she still had fun just by herself.

I smiled at Rita, put the bag on top of the violin case, and opened it again. And again Rita hurtled inside, so violently that she and the bag shot off the case and rolled on the ground. Faint squeaks of outrage came from inside the bag. Holly and I both laughed.

"Shhh! You sound like a couple of maniacs down there!" scolded Fourth Brother. I hadn't heard him come downstairs again. He put the dish of milk down. "Second Sister might hear you if you laugh like this."

"What took you so long?" I asked.

"Well, Second Sister saw me pouring out the milk," he said, "and I had to explain to her that practicing made me thirsty. Luckily she didn't ask me why I was planning to drink the milk out of a saucer."

Together we watched Rita lapping hungrily at the milk.

"You shouldn't give cats too much milk," warned Holly. "They can get sick from it, so you should just give it as a special treat. You'd better buy some cat food for Rita as soon as you get a chance. Krazy Kat is the best kind."

I began to worry. I could imagine what would

happen when I went to the grocery store with Mother and put a can of cat food into the shopping cart.

"What's that?" Mother would ask.

"It's Krazy Kat."

"Crazy what?"

"It's a kind of cat food," I'd have to admit.

"You mean we have to buy some special food for the *cat*?" I could imagine Mother's voice rising. "We barely have enough money to feed the *humans* in our family!"

Money was tight, since Father was a substitute violinist in the Seattle Symphony Orchestra — that is, he played only when one of the regular violinists couldn't make it. Father earned some extra money by giving lessons, but it wasn't much. His students were young beginners whose parents weren't ready to spend a lot of money on lessons.

Well, I'd have to do some more baby-sitting and earn enough to support Rita. She was my responsibility, not Father's.

Rita stopped before the milk was finished, and she began to wash her face. "Isn't that sweet?" I murmured. "Human babies aren't so tidy!"

Holly looked around the basement again.

"You've got a problem here. How will you make Rita come when it's feeding time? The basement is awfully large, and she has lots of corners where she can hide."

"How do you get your mother cat to come?" I asked.

"Well, I've trained her to come when I call her name," replied Holly.

"But if we're always yelling 'Rita, Rita,' somebody might overhear us," objected Fourth Brother. "They'll wonder who Rita is."

I thought about the problem. "High pitch carries well," I said finally. "We should make some sort of high sound."

Fourth Brother and I think alike. We looked at each other as the same idea occurred to both of us.

4

You mean the screeching of a violin, don't you?" Fourth Brother said excitedly.

I nodded. "We told Second Sister you were planning to practice violin in the basement. So nobody should be surprised if they hear some screeching down here."

Anyone else would have been insulted at the way I described his violin playing, but not Fourth Brother. "The screeching part will be easy," he said. "The hard part is pretending to be seriously practicing."

"You can play a certain tune every time we bring food," I said eagerly, carried away by my brilliant idea. "Then Rita will know that it means dinner, and she'll come running!"

Fourth Brother grimaced. "You're forgetting something: I can't play a tune — any tune."

That was true. But still, he could at least scratch out some sort of sound every time we brought food. "How about a rhythmic pattern on an open string? You can do that at least."

Fourth Brother's problem is with pitch: He can't tell high from low. But he has a good sense of rhythm, good enough to play the triangle in our school orchestra.

Holly was staring at us as we discussed our plan. "Say, that's pretty good!" she said. "It's just like Pavlov and his dog."

Holly was actually admiring *me*! I was so happy I wanted to sing. "Who is Pavlov, and what did his dog do?" I asked.

"He was a Russian scientist," Holly explained. "He played a bell every time he fed his dog. After a while, his dog would drool whenever he rang the bell, even without the food."

"I wouldn't do something cruel like that to you, Rita," I promised, stroking the kitten until her back arched up under my fingers.

"Okay," said Fourth Brother. "Let's try it with Rita."

He went and got his violin. Pulling the bow across the E string, he played a *di-di-di-dah* pattern. I shuddered as his bow slid at the end and made a screech. Rita's fur stood up and she

backed away, hissing.

She looked so funny that I had to laugh again.
Before she could run away, I picked her up and
nuzzled my face in her soft fur. "Did you hear
that, Rita? That *di-di-di-dah* pattern, followed
by a screech, means food!"

"I think it'll work," said Holly, smiling.
"Now, I've got to run. Good luck, Mary!"

At the front door she waved at me as she left.
I was so happy that I immediately ran upstairs,
took out my cello, and played a jig in double
time.

"What was that for?" asked Second Sister, coming into the room.

"I think I've made a new friend," I said.

From then on, Fourth Brother played his *di-di-di-dah* and screech every time we brought milk or cat food down to Rita. She was a smart cat, and she learned quickly. In less than a week, we got Rita to appear as soon as Fourth Brother's violin sounded.

I quickly found out that canned cat food cost more than I had thought, and almost all the money I earned baby-sitting went into feeding Rita. Plus Mother was starting to wonder why I was so eager to go to the grocery store.

"I really don't need anything today, Ying-mei," she told me. "Why don't you stay home and practice your new piece, the Bach sonata?"

"We're almost out of milk," I insisted. "Fourth Brother needs milk to grow tall and strong, so he can hit a home run for his team."

Mother looked unconvinced. "Seeing how fast the milk disappears in this house, I'm expecting him to turn into Wu Song!"

Wu Song is a storybook hero who is eight feet tall and kills a tiger with his bare hands. As I ran out of the house, I giggled at the thought of my little brother, Sprout, killing a tiger with his bare hands.

The rest of the family began to notice our frequent trips to the basement. They were also getting pretty tired of hearing *di-di-di-dah*, followed by a screech.

One evening, Fourth Brother was on his way to the basement stairs when Father stopped him. "Yingtao, you don't have to play your violin down there. Why don't you practice in the living room? I'll teach you a new tune."

"Yes, it's cold and dark in the basement," added Mother. "Stay up here where it's nice and warm."

Fourth Brother shook his head and looked

brave. "I know how much it hurts your ears to listen to me. I'll play in the basement until I improve."

As he clumped down the stairs, I could hear Second Sister's voice saying softly, "Poor boy. It's really touching that he's trying to play again. I suppose we should be more encouraging."

"I'll go down and help him with a little coaching," I said brightly. "It might cheer him up."

"Why don't *you* coach him?" Father said to Eldest Brother. "After all, you're the violinist."

"No, no!" I cried desperately. Everybody stared at me. I tried to think of a way to stop Eldest Brother. "Uh — well, you see, your standards are so high, Eldest Brother, that you make Fourth Brother nervous. He's not afraid of me, so he'll play better when I'm with him."

Eldest Brother sat down again. "I never knew I made him nervous," he muttered. He didn't insist, however. In fact he had been looking rather glum all evening.

Unexpectedly, Second Sister supported me. "Third Sister and Fourth Brother have always been close, and she can help him — if anybody can."

"That's right!" I agreed quickly. "I'll just go down and see how he's doing. In fact I'll bring him a snack to cheer him up. What he needs is a saucer of milk — er — I mean — a glass of milk."

I put a couple of fortune cookies on a saucer and poured a glass of milk. Without meeting any more objections from my family, I reached the basement stairs. Halfway down, I heard Fourth Brother's violin give its usual signal, and I braced myself, waiting for the screech. Sure enough, it came, and it sounded more piercing than usual.

At the bottom of the stairs I saw a sudden flurry, and there was Rita ready and waiting. I quickly removed the fortune cookies from the saucer and poured the milk into it. She was nudging my hand by the time I put down the saucer. For such a tiny kitten, she certainly made a loud lapping noise as she drank up the milk.

I broke open my fortune cookie, and the message said, "An unexpected friendship." I wondered if it meant my friendship with Holly. But I was already making progress. Could it still count as unexpected?

"That's that," said Fourth Brother with relief as he put away his violin. "I won't have to touch the fiddle until Rita's next meal."

He broke open the other cookie; his fortune read, "Success is the reward of effort." Fourth Brother shook his head. "My violin playing will never be a success, no matter how much effort I put into it."

"Maybe the cookie is talking about your effort in baseball," I told him. "It will be spring in a couple of months, and the baseball season will start. Besides, I don't think you put much effort into your violin playing. Do you have to make the screech quite so loud?"

"I was afraid Rita might not hear me otherwise," he said. "What's wrong? Is the family complaining?"

"They're pretty tired of hearing the same old thing," I told him. "That's *di-di-di-dah* plus a screech three times a day, and everyone is beginning to wonder when you'll move on to a new piece."

Fourth Brother grinned. "Don't worry. They know I'll never learn a piece of music no matter how many times I practice."

This was exactly what Second Sister said to me later when we were in our room getting ready for bed. "You know, maybe we should tell Fourth Brother that he will never learn to play the violin, no matter how much he practices," she said, taking off her cloth shoes and staring at the holes. "It's cruel to let him torture himself like this."

What she probably meant was that it was cruel to let him torture *us* like this. I looked at her innocently. "He'll never be as good as Eldest Brother. But he has the right to try, at least."

Thinking of Eldest Brother reminded me of his moodiness at dinner. "Did something happen today?" I asked. "Eldest Brother wasn't himself tonight."

Second Sister sighed and pulled the covers up to her nose. She likes to snuggle deep, a habit she's had as long as I can remember. Our apartment in China didn't have heating, and in winter even our noses got cold.

Finally I heard Second Sister's soft voice. "Eldest Brother had trouble with some boys in his class today. They were jeering at him and calling him a wimp. One of the boys tripped him, making him drop his violin on the ground. Fortunately it wasn't damaged."

I knew what a wimp was: It was on my list of English words. A wimp was a boy who spent all his time on music and studying and never joined in any of the sports.

"I wish Eldest Brother would take up baseball," I sighed. "Look how popular Fourth Brother is, now that he's a star on his baseball team."

"Fourth Brother plays baseball because he can't play the violin," Second Sister said acidly. "Now shut up and let me sleep!"

I stayed awake long after she had gone to sleep. My heart ached for Eldest Brother. I admired him so much, and I wanted others to admire him, too. Why was he so stubborn? Why couldn't he at least *try* sports?

Eventually I must have fallen asleep. The next thing I knew, Second Sister was hissing at me. "What's that noise?" she demanded.

I sat up and listened. After a while I heard some thin squeaks. Rita! She must be meowing! Maybe she was lonely and wanted petting.

I jumped out of bed. "I'll go and see. The noise seems to be coming from downstairs."

Second Sister got up, too. "I'll go with you." She was shivering. She's thinner than I am, so she feels the cold a lot more.

"You go back to bed," I urged. "I can go by myself."

She hesitated. Her shivering grew worse.

"Aren't you scared to go alone?" she asked shakily.

"There's nothing to be afraid of," I said. Of course I wasn't afraid, since I knew perfectly well that it was Rita making the noise.

Second Sister was reassured. Besides, she was getting very cold. "All right. But yell if you think you need help."

I crept downstairs as quietly as I could. Someone had left the basement door open, and that was why Rita's meows could be heard upstairs. I hurried down to the basement and found her trying to climb the stairs. She was too small to make it, but one of these days — maybe very soon — she would manage. Then what were we going to do?

I decided to worry about that when the time came. Meanwhile, I picked up the kitten and crooned to her. She was purring when I put her back in her box. I wanted to stay and play with her, to keep her company, to show her I hadn't forgotten her. She was lonely there in the dark basement, all by herself.

Then I remembered that cats don't mind the dark. I hardened myself and went back up the stairs. As I clicked the door shut, something loomed up in front of me and I choked back a scream.

"What are you doing up at this time of night?" demanded Eldest Brother's voice.

"I — I — thought I heard some squeaks," I stammered.

"Maybe we have rats," said Fourth Brother's voice. He was standing behind Eldest Brother.

That gave me an idea. "Yes, it certainly sounded like rats. I know what: We'll get a cat!"

Eldest Brother turned away. "You know perfectly well we can't have a cat. We don't have room for one, and besides it would tear up our music. Father would never allow it."

I sighed and followed him upstairs. Behind me I heard Fourth Brother's sigh as well.

By taking Rita, I had thought I was getting closer to Holly. I was definitely counted as part of her group now, and when I saw her in school, it was perfectly natural for me to join her and talk about the kitten.

One day, we had finished lunch and still had a few minutes before the bell. I went over to Holly and, as usual, reported on Rita's latest progress. "You should see the way she comes streaking the minute my brother plays his violin! It took her no time to learn that meant food."

Holly laughed. "I guess she likes her 'dinner music.' "

"That's a good idea, Mary," said Kim. I was surprised. For the first time, Kim was saying something friendly to me. "Cats are good at hearing high-pitch sounds like the violin."

"High pitch is right," I said. "My younger brother is playing for the cat, and he's a terrible violinist. The family is beginning to complain."

"Too bad you can't get your older brother to play instead," said Kim. "Jason says he's the best violinist in their school orchestra."

"He's the concert master," I said. I always felt a glow of pride when Eldest Brother was mentioned.

"Apparently he's the best violinist because he spends every second practicing his violin," said Kim. "Jason says your brother does nothing else at all — nothing!"

"Oh, come on," I protested. "My brother eats and sleeps. He even sneezes, sometimes."

"Well, the kids in Jason's class think your brother is a real wimp."

Suddenly Kim didn't seem so friendly any

more. Jason was Kim's elder brother, and I began to suspect that he was one of the boys who had taunted Eldest Brother and tripped him.

I began to tremble with anger and got up abruptly. "Excuse me, I see someone over there I have to talk to."

I joined some girls who were jumping rope and tried to stop thinking about the hateful things Kim had said. Earlier, I had thought that I might even get to be friends with her. She could be really funny sometimes, and I liked the way she rolled her eyes, inviting everyone to laugh along with her.

She was probably jealous of me because I was becoming better friends with Holly. I had to be careful and make sure she didn't turn Holly against me. Also, she might tell Jason about the kitten, and the news could reach Eldest Brother. From now on, Kim was the enemy.

5

Eldest Brother keeps his carpentry tools in the basement, and I was always afraid he might catch sight of Rita when he went down to get something. I put her box in a dark corner farthest away from where his toolbox was, but she was very curious, always sniffing around. What if she came over to investigate the toolbox just when Eldest Brother was down there? Every time he went to the basement, Fourth Brother and I would look nervously at each other.

"There's a funny smell in the basement," Eldest Brother said one day after he had gone down to get his hammer. "Maybe I should give the place a thorough cleaning. All sorts of garbage might be lying around down there."

"Oh, you don't have to do that!" Fourth Brother and I said at the same time.

We both grinned foolishly. Then I turned to Eldest Brother. "You've got a concert coming up in school, and you have to practice for that solo. We'll clean up the basement for you!"

Eldest Brother looked amazed. Not since history began had we ever volunteered to do any housecleaning. But he didn't argue. He wasn't all that enthusiastic about cleaning up a big, dark basement full of rubbish.

That night, Fourth Brother and I went down to the basement as usual for his "violin practice." After he had played his *di-di-di-dah* and screech, Rita streaked over with her usual incredible speed.

I sniffed around. "You know, Eldest Brother is right: It does smell bad down here."

As we watched Rita eating, Fourth Brother said, "The smell must be coming from her box of dirt!"

He was right. I went over to the box that we had filled with dirt so Rita could use it as her toilet.

Rita was quite neat in covering her waste. But after many days of use, the dirt definitely smelled.

"We have to change it more often," I said, sighing. "Maybe every day."

The next day I went into the garden and dumped out the box of Rita's dirt. While I was digging up fresh soil, Second Sister came over to watch me. "I miss the vegetables we had in China," she sighed. "What are you planting?"

I tried to think of something. "Uh — how about some bok choy?"

Bok choy is a deep green vegetable we used to eat a lot, since it was both plentiful and cheap. Here in America, it's available but fairly expensive, so we had been eating cheaper things like cabbage. Once in a while, Mother bought greens in Chinatown for a special treat.

Second Sister looked delighted. "That's wonderful, Third Sister!"

I began to feel guilty. "It's almost winter, so I'll have to wait until spring before I can plant anything," I muttered. "I'm just getting the ground ready."

"I miss those fields with green vegetables," Second Sister said dreamily. "I even miss the smell of dung that farmers put on their fields. And remember those strings of ducks waddling across the footpaths?"

She still suffered homesickness for China, and sometimes she would play Chinese folk songs on her viola. She always seemed to pick the gloomiest ones. Once, when Father heard me grumbling, he scolded, "Yingmei, Second Sister misses China more than you do, so you have to be understanding. Anyway, we shouldn't forget the songs of our old home."

When I saw the wistful look on Second Sister's face, I promised myself that I'd really plant green vegetables next spring. At least our soil here would be fertilized — very well fertilized!

Second Sister would get suspicious if she saw me constantly digging in the garden, though. Next day in school I confessed to Holly that I had been using dirt from the garden for Rita, but it was getting awfully smelly. "I'd better buy kitty litter after all."

Holly nodded approval. "Make sure you get the brand called Kitten Fresh. It has some special stuff that deodorizes. You won't have to change it as often as garden soil."

Holly was glad to give me advice about Rita, and I tried to follow her directions faithfully. Right after school I hurried to the grocery store. The price for Kitten Fresh took my breath away. It cost $4.69 for one bag! At this rate, I'd have to baby-sit every night to earn enough money for taking care of Rita. I wouldn't have any money left for spending on other things I wanted — first on the list was a pair of sneakers just like Holly's.

For a moment I wondered if I couldn't keep on using garden soil. But Holly said Americans buy this special material for their cats. I wanted to do everything right — everything that Americans did. And I had to prove to Holly that I cared as much about animals as she did.

Resigned, I bought the Kitten Fresh after all. Rita deserved the best, and the sneakers would just have to wait.

Eldest Brother kept peering around the house when he was home. One night, when I had just finished playing a duet with him, he suddenly jumped up and looked around wildly.

"What's the matter?" I asked.

"Don't you hear it?" he said. "That squeak?"

I listened, then shook my head. "I don't hear anything."

He sat down again and began to put his violin away. "It's stopped now. It sounded for a minute like a rusty door."

Rusty door? He must have been hearing Rita meowing!

"Maybe some of the doors in the house *are* rusty," I suggested. "After all, this is an old house, and we have to expect squeaks here and there."

"They get on my nerves," Eldest Brother said. "I'll ask Mr. Conner what I can do."

For rusty doors Mr. Conner recommended squirting lubricating oil into the hinges. Soon, we got used to the sight of Eldest Brother going around the house with a can of oil in his hand. Late at night was when he heard the squeaks most often, because that was when the house was the quietest.

I had an awful scare when I got up late to go to the bathroom. I turned a corner and saw Eldest Brother's figure looming up in front of me. I squeaked, and he was so startled that he squirted oil all over *me!*

As Rita grew bigger, her cries were sure to sound deeper. Right now she sounded like a squeaky door, but what could I tell Eldest Brother when Rita eventually made a really loud *meow?*

I felt bad that Rita was making Eldest Brother so jumpy. He was playing a solo piece at the high school winter concert the next day, and he needed his rest. I hoped he wouldn't be too tired to play well.

Our whole family went to the high school concert. Eldest Brother's solo was a piece by Paganini, and in spite of his jumpiness, he played beautifully. Listening to him, I was so proud that I felt tears come into my eyes.

Afterward, when we were getting ready to go home, some of the kids and their parents came over to congratulate Eldest Brother. To my surprise, Kim brought her family over to meet us. Her parents, Mr. and Mrs. O'Meara, shook hands with my parents. "You must be very

proud to have such a talented son," said Mrs. O'Meara.

While the grown-ups were talking, Kim's brother, Jason, came over. "So this is the talented Yang family," he said to Eldest Brother. "I hear you're all musical geniuses."

It didn't sound like a compliment, the way he said it. Eldest Brother only said quietly, "We practice a lot, that's all."

Jason's lips curled. "Yeah, I bet. Say, don't you try sports at all? How about Ping-Pong, at least?"

Eldest Brother shook his head. "I'm afraid I might injure one of my fingers."

Jason had to cover his mouth, but even behind his palm I could hear him sputter with laughter.

Next to him, Kim stared at Eldest Brother with round eyes. "Around here, if a guy isn't into sports, people will start calling him a nerd," she said finally. "Doesn't that bother you?"

Eldest Brother shook his head. "I can't pretend to be athletic when I'm not."

"Wow," Kim said, almost in a whisper.

I was sure that by tomorrow, Kim would tell all our friends that my brother didn't dare play Ping-Pong in case he hurt a finger. Everyone would be sniggering and calling him a nerd.

After we got home that night, I went into the kitchen to get a saucer of milk. Eldest Brother was there, inspecting the kitchen cabinet doors. He swung them back and forth one by one, to see which one squeaked.

"Eldest Brother, why *don't* you take up a sport?" I asked. "You have good coordination. You could be a really good athlete."

He squirted some oil into the hinge of a lower

cabinet door. "You heard what I told Jason. I don't want to injure a finger."

"Yes, but you're always doing carpentry work. Didn't you hit a finger with a hammer last month? You played all those dazzling runs with the finger bandaged, and you did fine!"

He smiled. "Athletics won't mend our broken front step."

I sighed. Why didn't Eldest Brother try a little harder to make people respect him? If he would only make more of an effort to fit in, others would admire him as much as I did, wouldn't they?

6

Every member of my family had done things to embarrass me in front of my friends — everyone except Father. He didn't call people old and fat. He didn't wear cloth shoes with holes in them. Nobody called him Sprout or a wimp. All our neighbors and friends respected him. I thought at least *he* was safe — until the PTA bake sale.

The PTA was raising money for an aquarium in the school library. When I told my family about this, they thought it was an excellent idea. "It's much better than keeping fish in the bathtub," said Mother. "Every time I buy live fish for dinner, none of us can take a bath that day."

"The school isn't going to use the aquarium for food fish," I explained. "It's for beautiful tropical fish."

"It must be like a zoo, then," remarked Second Sister, "except that it will be for fish."

We all agreed that it was a luxury for our school to have its own zoo for fish. Truly, America was a rich country.

I asked Mother if she could contribute something to sell. I had cut out a recipe from the newspaper for chocolate chip cookies. After looking over the lunch boxes of my friends, I decided that was what American kids liked best. I wanted people to know that my mother could bake normal, American food if she wanted to.

Instead, Mother decided to make fried wontons. "I don't need a recipe for these," she explained.

Second Sister usually helps Mother when she cooks, but this time I helped her wrap the wontons. Here in Seattle, we can buy ready-made wonton skins, which taste as good as any in China. We make our own filling of ground meat seasoned with soy sauce and chopped green onions. For myself, I prefer fried wontons to cookies, but I was worried my classmates might feel different.

The PTA bake sale was held at the school gymnasium. Mother unwrapped her dish and set it down on one of the long tables, together with plates of pies, cakes, and cookies. Next to all these sweets, the wontons looked so weird that I was afraid nobody would want to buy any.

But when my teacher saw Mother's dish, she was delighted. "I was hoping somebody would bring some ethnic food!" she exclaimed.

Mother looked startled. "This is just ordinary, everyday food," she protested.

There are many ethnic minorities in China: Mongols, Yi, Miao . . . My family had always loved their beautiful costumes and exotic dances. But we had never thought of *ourselves* as ethnic.

"We're studying America's multicultural heritage in our history classes," continued my teacher. "Your dish of wontons represents one of the many ethnic strands that make up our country."

Mother still looked puzzled, but I immediately took out my notebook to enter the words *multicultural* and *ethnic*.

Mother's fried wontons turned out to be a hit at the bake sale. Listening to the other parents praise Mother's dish and watching her beaming face, I felt really proud of her. This was the first time I was proud of her being the way she was, instead of wishing she could act more like my friends' parents.

Soon Kim came to the bake sale with her parents. Mrs. O'Meara put down a tray of things that looked like small, flat breads. I wanted to ask Kim what they were, but after what her brother had said about Eldest Brother, I wasn't sure I wanted to talk to her.

But Kim smiled pleasantly at me and said, "Hi, Mary."

Well, maybe she could answer some of my questions after all. "What is 'multicultural'?" I asked.

Kim rolled her eyes and thought. "I guess it means coming from different backgrounds — you know, different ethnic groups."

"What about those things your mother made?" I asked. "Are they ethnic, too?"

Mrs. O'Meara was listening to our conversation. "Those are Irish soda biscuits, Mary, and O'Meara is a good Irish name," she said, smiling. "So I guess these biscuits are ethnic."

"How about Holly?" I asked.

Mr. O'Meara joined us. "Hey, Hanson is a Swedish name. That makes Holly ethnic, too."

Everybody laughed. I joined in, but I didn't get the joke. Secretly, I suspected that some people were more ethnic than others.

Mr. O'Meara began to chat with Father. "Whereabouts is your hometown in China?" he asked.

"My ancestral home is in Jiangsu," said Father. "It's in the central eastern part of China."

"Do you grow a lot of rice there?" asked Mrs. O'Meara.

"Yes," said Father. "The land there is very fertile. Where we live, the lice glows near the liver."

Mrs. O'Meara's eyes grew round. She stared

at Father for a moment, then went into a fit of giggles.

When Father speaks English, his accent is pretty good. He has a good ear, since he's a professional musician, after all. His English always has the right melody, and from the next room it sounds perfect. But he has a lot of trouble with English consonants. He can't pronounce the *th* sound, because it doesn't exist in Chinese. When he tries to say "lather," he ends up saying "ladder." His worst enemy is the letter *r*, which he pronounces like *l*. What he'd been trying to say just then was "The rice grows near the river."

Now the entire Yang family had managed to embarrass me in public. At least Holly and her mother weren't here to witness our disgrace.

Mrs. Hanson and Holly arrived at the bake sale just too late to hear Father's lice and liver. But would he say something even worse? To my relief, Father said he had to play in a concert that night, and left before he could mangle any more English consonants.

Mrs. Hanson had not seen Mother since that painful Thanksgiving dinner, when Mother had complimented her on being old and fat. Mrs. Hanson seemed quite willing to forgive and forget, however. She bought the remaining wontons and told Mother they looked simply delicious.

In addition to worrying about my family's behavior, I was afraid Mrs. Hanson might mention something about Rita. I got nervous when I heard her ask, "Do you have a yard, Mrs. Yang?"

"Why, yes," Mother replied. "We live in a duplex, and we share the yard with the Sylvesters, an elderly couple next door. But I don't have much time to do any gardening. Fortunately Yingmei likes the garden."

Mrs. Hanson looked puzzled. "Who is Ying-mei?"

"That's me," I said quickly. "That's my Chinese name. But my American friends all call me Mary."

"Yingmei spends a lot of time digging in the garden," said Mother, smiling at me fondly and making me feel guilty.

"If you have a garden," Mrs. Hanson said, "then you do have room for a pet."

I didn't like the way the conversation was going. "Mother is a pianist, Mrs. Hanson," I said feverishly. "She's very good at sight reading, and she can play just about any music without having to practice."

Holly caught my eye and smiled faintly. She knew why I was trying to steer the conversation away from pets. "If we ever need an accompanist in a hurry, Mom," she murmured, "we could ask Mrs. Yang to play."

"Yes, of course," said Mrs. Hanson. "But getting back to the subject of pets . . ."

I had to interrupt, even if it was rude. "Mrs. Hanson works in the records business, Mother. Maybe they need pianists sometimes!"

There was a silence. Nobody seemed to know what I was talking about.

Then Holly laughed. "You've got it wrong, Mary. Mom works at the records department of a hospital. It means she keeps files on all the patients. She doesn't have anything to do with making recordings."

I could feel the heat rising from my neck to my face and scalp — maybe even reaching the ends of my hair. In spite of all my hard work in writing down new English expressions, there were still some that tripped me up! But at least it got Mrs. Hanson away from the dangerous subject of pets.

Mother was interested in Mrs. Hanson's job, and wanted to know more about what it was like to work in a hospital. For a while they chatted in a friendly way, and I began to relax.

"Why don't we look around at some of the other tables," suggested Holly. "There are lots of goodies left."

"Sure!" I said happily. Holly and I started to walk off together — almost like best friends. As usual, I told Holly about Rita. "I went and bought a big bag of Kitten Fresh."

Holly nodded approval. "That's the best kind. It's a bit more expensive than other brands, but it's worth the extra cost."

Kim, chomping on a chocolate chip cookie, followed us. "Still talking about Rita?"

"Holly can teach me a lot about animals, and I have so much to learn," I said humbly. Even to my own ears, my words sounded disgustingly like flattery.

"You haven't told your parents about Rita yet?" asked Kim.

"I'm planning to tell them very soon," I said, with more confidence than I felt.

"You know," Kim said slowly, "I can take Rita if your parents won't let you keep her. Jason is allergic to cats, but if I keep Rita brushed, her hair won't get on any of the furniture."

"I think it's better if Mary keeps Rita," said Holly. "She has already bonded with the kitten."

I didn't know what "bonded" meant, but it sounded very technical — just the sort of thing a future veterinarian would know. Kim's face fell, and she left us. I knew why she had suggested taking Rita. For a moment I even felt sorry for her.

Holly and I went back to the table where Mother was standing with Mrs. Hanson. They were still talking about Mrs. Hanson's job.

When we came up to them, Mother was saying, "Your work sounds absolutely fascinating, Mrs. Hanson. What is your salary?"

I smothered a groan. I knew that talking about money is bad manners here and that asking about someone's salary is even worse.

Mrs. Hanson's face froze again. Finally she said, "My salary is my own business, Mrs. Yang." She turned and beckoned to Holly. "We'd better go home."

I looked desperately at Holly for support. She at least might understand that this was just another case of the differences between Chinese and American customs. But she didn't even look at me. She simply followed her mother and left the school.

Slowly, I went over to Mother and took up the empty plate, which had a few crumbs of wonton skins. Neither of us could think of anything to say.

My teacher came over and congratulated Mother. "Everybody is saying what a treat your fried wontons were! Isn't this a great bake sale?"

She rushed off without waiting for a reply, which was good. I for one wasn't up to making one. My throat felt thick, and I wanted to cry.

Mother and I walked home silently. A block

from our house, Mother stopped. "I'm sorry, Yingmei. I know that you want to be friends with Holly, but I always seem to be saying things that offend her mother."

I had to clear my throat several times before I could reply. "It's not your fault, Mother."

But it *is* her fault, I said to myself. Why didn't she try harder to learn about American customs? I spent all my time learning how things were done in this country. I kept my list of new words and practiced them every day. I wouldn't say something awful every time I opened my mouth!

7

Not only was Mrs. Hanson offended, but now even Holly seemed fed up with our family. She probably wouldn't want to speak to me again.

After this, taking the kitten wouldn't be enough to save my friendship with Holly. All that work, worry, and expense had been wasted. Besides, my parents would soon find out about Rita anyway and make me give her up.

The first sign of trouble came from the Sylvesters. "Hi, Mary," said Mr. Sylvester one day when I came home from school. "I keep seeing a kitten coming to our yard. Do you know who it belongs to?"

He sounded wistful. "Jenny wants another dog," he continued. "She sure misses Benny, but I kind of like the idea of a kitten. Less

trouble than a dog, you know?"

Suddenly his eyes widened. "There she goes!
Cute, isn't she?"

I looked at where he was pointing. It was Rita!
How did she get out of the basement?

I had to get her back, and the only way was to have Fourth Brother play his special tune. I muttered something to Mr. Sylvester, then turned and hurried to the Conners' house. Fourth Brother was there, going over some homework problems with Matthew.

"What's the matter, Mary?" asked Matthew, who opened the door.

I took a deep breath. "Fourth Brother has to come home right away and play the violin!"

Matthew's jaw dropped. "I thought he'd given it up. If you really need a fiddler, maybe I can come and play."

Fourth Brother appeared. "That's okay, Matthew. I'd better go home. There's a piece that only I can play."

Matthew's jaw dropped farther. It was practically touching his stomach. "This I've got to hear!"

"No, you don't want to hear!" I cried. I turned to Fourth Brother, who was already putting his jacket on. "Come on, we have to hurry!"

"What happened?" asked Fourth Brother as we ran. "Is it Rita?"

"Yes," I panted. "Somehow she escaped from the basement, and Mr. Sylvester saw her in the garden. You've got to play your violin and get her back!"

We rushed back into the house, and Fourth Brother took his violin out. Just as we reached the door to the basement, Father appeared. "Practicing again, Yingtao? Good, good!" He tried to sound hearty, but the strain showed.

"Yes, Father," Fourth Brother said humbly. "I'd better get to work right away."

Before he could go down the steps, Father stopped him. "Er . . . Yingtao . . . that phrase you've been practicing . . . I know you want to do it perfectly, but you really need some help. Let me show you."

He took up Fourth Brother's violin, and frowned when he ran his fingers over the strings. "This is appallingly out of tune! No wonder you sound so awful!"

Father tuned the violin, then handed it back to Fourth Brother. "Now try that phrase."

Fourth Brother gulped. He slowly put the instrument under his chin, and he slowly drew the bow across the E string. *Di-di-di-dah*, he played. Only he played it so slowly that it sounded more like *duh duh duh dooh*.

Father winced. I winced. I had caught sight

of a streak in the backyard. It was Rita, and she had heard the dinner call. The next instant, she disappeared.

Fourth Brother hung his head. "Father, I really think I'd better practice in the basement."

Somberly Father nodded. He gave a deep sigh as he watched Fourth Brother march down the basement steps.

"I'll go and keep his spirits up," I said.

"You're a good girl, Yingmei," Father said, putting his hand on my shoulder. "You've always been such a great help to Yingtao."

I was just about to go down the stairs when Eldest Brother came in. "It's funny," he said, shaking his head. "When I was walking across the yard, I nearly tripped over some sort of animal."

"It must have been a rat!" I said.

"It seemed too big for a rat," said Eldest Brother.

"Rats get very big in America," I said eagerly, "because the garbage here is so rich. We really need a cat."

It didn't work. Father shook his head. "You know very well that we can't have a cat."

Di-di-di-dah, *screech* went the sound of Fourth

Brother's violin.

"Er . . . there's some music I have to mark," Father said, and hurried upstairs to the second floor.

"I have — uh — some music to mark as well," said Eldest Brother quickly, and followed Father.

I put some Krazy Kat into a dish, and when I got down to the basement, Rita was already there, circling around Fourth Brother's ankles. Both of them looked impatient.

"How did she get in and out, anyway?" asked Fourth Brother as we stood and watched Rita gobbling up the food.

"She must have found some kind of opening leading to the yard. We'll have to close it up."

We tried to find the opening, but we didn't see it anywhere. There were a couple of heavy, rusty trunks in one corner. "Maybe there's a hole in the wall behind these trunks," I said, trying to move one of them aside.

Fourth Brother tried to help me, but even with the two of us together, we couldn't make it budge. "If the opening is behind here, there isn't a thing we can do about it," I sighed.

"You know, we can't keep Rita hidden down

here forever," said Fourth Brother, dusting his hands off. "The secret is bound to come out. Why don't we tell the others?"

I bit my lower lip to prevent it from quivering. "Then they'll send Rita away! You heard Father. She'd tear up our sheet music and scratch our instruments." Plus, I said to myself, Holly would never forgive me if Rita ended up drowned in the pond.

"We'll just have to keep our instruments in our cases," said Fourth Brother, "and put the music out of reach somewhere."

"That's easy enough for *you* to say," I objected. "You hardly touch your violin except to play the dinner tune."

"Let's try, at least."

So I tried. Whenever I saw one of our instruments lying on a sofa or on the floor, I'd put it away in its case and snap the lid shut. Soon this became a real bother, and the worst was my cello. It isn't too hard to put a violin or viola back in its case. But my cello has a canvas cover, and it isn't easy to insert the spike at the bottom through the little hole in the cloth and zip up the sides. Things would be easier if I had a hard case like the others, but a hard case for a cello is much too expensive.

My mania for neatness surprised the family. "Where's my viola?" demanded Second Sister after dinner one night. When I told her I had put it back in the case, her eyebrows shot up. "Whatever for?"

"Well," I muttered, "I thought our living room would look better without all this mess."

"We don't have a mess! We have music and we have instruments."

"After all, Father's students have their lessons here, and it would make a better impression if everything was put away."

"The impression we make is that we're musical," retorted Second Sister. "What's wrong with that? It's the truth!"

She stared at me for a moment. "I know. You just want us to make a good impression on your friend Holly, don't you?"

Our family had already made an impression on Holly, and it wasn't a good one. So I just shook my head.

Second Sister stared harder. "You can't become friends with Holly by pretending to be something you aren't. You want her to think we have a neat house and our family is just like other Americans, but it won't work, you know."

I couldn't meet her eyes, because I didn't

want to admit that what she said was true. I just looked down.

Unexpectedly, Eldest Brother supported me. "It might not be a bad thing to put away our instruments and protect them from the sun and dust."

I got an idea. "Eldest Brother, can you build a shelf for our music? I nearly stepped on your score yesterday."

Fourth Brother poked me, but even without his warning, I had seen the danger myself. It was already too late.

"That's a great idea!" exclaimed Eldest Brother. He was so enthusiastic that he went over right away to the Conners' house to borrow some wood.

Fourth Brother looked at me reproachfully. "You know what will happen, don't you? Eldest Brother will be working in the basement, and Rita will come over to investigate. She loves company, and nothing will keep her away!"

"I know," I said miserably. "I'll have to think of some way to keep her out of sight."

It turned out to be much harder than I had expected. Eldest Brother began to work on the shelf after dinner the next day, and I followed him nervously down to the basement.

At first I thought the noise of the sawing scared Rita away, because there was no sign of her. Then, just as Eldest Brother put down one of the planks he had sawed, I caught sight of a little nose poking out from behind the furnace.

"Shoo, shoo!" I hissed, trying to wave her off.

"What did you say?" asked Eldest Brother.

I pretended to sneeze: "Tishoo!"

"It's chilly down here," said Eldest Brother. "You don't have to stay, Third Sister. I can manage by myself."

Rita pranced forward, eager to join us. I remembered the time at Holly's house when she tried to push her way into the circle of other kittens. I had felt sorry for her, because she had reminded me of myself. But this time I was only exasperated. When I tried to push her back, she got away and mewed at me.

Eldest Brother looked around. I quickly made mewing noises. "Mew . . . mew . . . mu . . . music is my life!" I sang desperately.

"You're acting awfully strange today," muttered Eldest Brother, picking up his pencil and marking the wooden plank.

Again Rita advanced. Quickly, I picked up one of the wooden planks and held it in front of the kitten. Eldest Brother looked around. "I'm not ready for that one yet."

"I'm just taking a sniff," I said quickly. "I *love* the smell of new wood!"

"Don't put your nose too close to it, or you might sneeze again," Eldest Brother said dryly.

I looked down and saw Rita's tail sticking out from the side of the plank. I hurriedly changed the position of the plank. Rita changed her position, too. Every time I moved the plank, she followed, and her tail still stuck out. She thought it was a wonderful new game.

"Would you stop waving that plank around?" growled Eldest Brother. "It's very distracting!"

Rita started to scratch the wood. She had found something fresh to sharpen her claws on. To hide the noise, I began to sing again. Looking down, I saw the tip of Rita's tail.

I lost my patience and did something really stupid: I stepped on her tail. To this day, I swear I didn't step very hard.

Rita howled. I howled, too — only louder.

Eldest Brother's saw shrieked. He threw it down and looked at the end of the plank in disgust. "It's split! The piece is going to be too short if I cut off the split part!"

He turned and glared at me. "How can I con-centrate if you make that horrible noise?"

"I'm sorry," I mumbled. "I hit my foot with the plank." I looked up at him. "You know, Eldest Brother, we can just put some bricks be-tween the planks for our shelf. Then you don't have to do any more sawing or hammering."

Eldest Brother looked only half convinced. He wanted more of a chance to use his carpentry skill. "Well, we'll talk about it tomorrow. Maybe Mr. Conner can give me another piece of wood."

As we started up the stairs, I saw something move from the corner of my eye. Eldest Brother did, too. "What was that?" he demanded.

I tried once again. "It was a rat! I keep telling you that we have lots of rats here. We really have to get a cat."

It was no use. Eldest Brother shook his head again.

At least that was the end of his carpentry proj-ect. We made shelves by putting the planks of wood between stacks of bricks, but it turned out that nobody put any music on them. We liked to leave the music open to the place we wanted, and besides, it was simply too much trouble.

After a couple of days, even *I* gave up trying to put away the instruments.

There was no way we could allow Rita to come upstairs. And yet she couldn't stay in the basement forever, either. Poor little thing, she was so lonely down there all by herself. I knew exactly how it felt to be left out. The trouble was that since Rita knew how to get out of the basement, she might run away one of these days.

Everything was going wrong for me. My friendship with Holly looked hopeless. My family kept embarrassing me in public. And Rita was becoming more of a problem every day.

I felt desperate.

8

After that embarrassing night at the PTA bake sale, I gave up trying to join Holly's circle during lunch and recess. Fourth Brother walked home from school with his friend Matthew, and I walked home by myself. It was pretty lonely.

A phone call changed all that. "Hello, is this Mary?" said a woman's voice. It sounded familiar. "This is Mrs. O'Meara — you know, Kim's mother. I'm calling to see if you can come to Kim's birthday party next Saturday."

I was so surprised that I almost dropped the phone. It was all I could do to stammer my acceptance.

After I had hung up the phone, I began to wonder why Mrs. O'Meara had invited me. I thought Kim didn't even like me. In fact, I thought she was jealous of my friendship with Holly.

The next day at lunch, I went over nervously to the table where Holly, Kim, and their friends sat. Holly greeted me in her usual way, her voice quiet and unexcited. Maybe she had forgotten about my parents' slips at the bake sale. Maybe she hadn't even noticed that I hadn't been eating lunch with them lately.

Actually, it was Kim I wanted to talk to. I sat down next to her. "Thanks for inviting me to your birthday party."

Kim rolled her eyes. I suddenly realized that she did that sometimes when she wanted to hide her embarrassment. "That's okay," she mumbled. "You're part of our group."

A warm glow began in my chest and spread all over me, until my face felt rosy. I was part of the group. I belonged.

Kim spoiled things by saying, "Besides, my parents wanted to invite you. They enjoyed meeting you and your folks the other day."

It was like being splashed with cold water. But Kim added, "I thought your brother's playing at the winter concert was wonderful. And he wasn't afraid of being called a nerd. I liked that."

I was so surprised that I just stared at her.

Before I could think of anything to say, Kim asked, "How is Rita?"

"She's growing fast!" I said. Then I remembered that Kim had wanted to take Rita. "Are you going to tell my family about her?"

"Of course not!" said Kim. "I'm no tattletale!"

I was instantly ashamed. "I'm sorry, Kim. That was mean of me."

"That's okay," Kim said gruffly. Suddenly she grinned. "Actually, I did think about it, but I figured your parents will find out soon enough anyway."

She was honest, at least. Talking to Kim was relaxing, because with her I didn't have to work hard to be better than I was.

I told her more about Rita, and Kim looked so wistful that I surprised myself by inviting her to come to our basement to play with the kitten.

"That's a neat idea," said Kim, "training the kitten to come at the sound of the violin. Mom could use a trick like that. She's always complaining that she has to yell herself hoarse to get Dad to the dinner table. He's incredibly absent-minded, you know, and doesn't hear you unless you call half a dozen times."

The school bell rang. "See you next Saturday," said Kim.

I had never been invited to a birthday party in America. In fact I had never been to a party where all the guests were young people. When I arrived at the O'Mearas' house Saturday evening, I didn't know what to expect. Would I disgrace myself, like the rest of my family? I took a deep breath and rang the bell.

Mrs. O'Meara opened the door. "Hi, Mary. Glad you could come. The others are here already."

While I was taking off my jacket, I saw that Mr. and Mrs. O'Meara were putting theirs on. "We're going out for dinner," explained Mrs. O'Meara. "You kids will have a better time without grown-ups looking over your shoulder."

I couldn't imagine this happening at a Chinese birthday party, where several generations of people would gather to celebrate together. I decided that I rather liked this American custom.

After Mr. and Mrs. O'Meara went out the door, I nervously entered the living room, where

Kim, Holly, and the other three girls in her circle were already sitting.

"Happy birthday, Kim," I said, handing her my gift.

The others greeted me, and I began to relax. I was in. I was accepted.

The living room was littered with torn wrapping paper. Kim had been opening her presents. I saw a T-shirt with a funny picture, a CD, and a couple of things that smelled good. I picked up a small bottle and saw that the label said "Bath Salts." Why would anyone want to salt the water when they took a bath? It was like making soup! I resolved to investigate this question privately as soon as I had a chance.

The other presents all looked store-bought, and I began to worry again. Since I'd been spending most of my money on Rita, I didn't have much left for Kim's present. I knew she played the flute, so I had taken the music for a Mozart flute quartet and had it photocopied. Then I had asked Second Sister to draw a picture for a cover.

Next to all these nice gifts, mine would look awfully cheap. But Kim seemed pleased by it. Flipping through the pages, she said, "Gee, it looks hard. You think I can play it?"

"Of course you can," I assured her, then added, "after you've practiced."

"But it's for four people," she said.

I nodded. "That's right. It's a quartet for flute, violin, viola, and cello. Maybe you can come to our house one of these days and play with us."

Kim blushed a little and looked even more pleased. "Your brother was so good at his school concert! I'd be scared to play with him."

"Don't worry," I said. "My brother can take a lot of punishment."

Then I realized that this sounded insulting. I was talking about Fourth Brother, of course, but Kim might think I was talking about her. She didn't seem to mind, though, and continued to look at the music. She also liked Second Sister's cover.

I breathed a sigh of relief.

"Remember your last birthday, Kim?" sighed Debbie. "It was great! We played Spoons and all those other wacky games!"

"I like eating supper here by ourselves and going to the movies afterward," said Holly. "It seems more grown-up."

Jill, one of the other girls, immediately agreed. "That's right. We're too old for playing games."

"Since my mom and dad are going out for dinner, we're ordering pizza," said Kim. "What kind should we get?"

Everyone looked excited. "I like pepperoni," said Debbie.

"I like the Hawaiian pizza, with ham and pineapple," said Jill.

"A mushroom pizza would be good," suggested Holly. "Mushrooms aren't so salty, so they don't clash with the cheese."

"Yeah, good idea," Debbie said quickly.

Everybody else agreed right away, too. Kim went to the phone and called up Pizza Barn to deliver a large mushroom pizza with extra cheese.

I began to notice something. Although it was Kim's birthday, Holly was the center of attention, the way she always was at school. The others all followed her lead in ordering the pizza, and they listened to her when she said that playing games at birthday parties was too childish. I did it, too. Even though I liked music, I only talked about animals with Holly because that was what she was interested in.

Why was Holly always the leader? Why did the others admire her so much? I knew why *I* wanted to be her friend. She was the princess on my candy box, calm and sure of herself. But how did she get the rest of the group to do what she wanted?

I didn't have much time to wonder about this, because the pizza delivery man rang the doorbell. I had heard about pizzas, but I had never tried one, and I had no idea it could be delivered so fast. At last I would find out what it tasted like.

In northern China, people eat a big, flat, round bread. It's pretty cheap compared to other kinds of food; it's mostly dough, with a few chopped green onions, sesame seeds, and bits of egg or dried shrimps to add flavor.

I was amazed at the amount of stuff on top of the pizza. The layer of mushrooms, cheese, and tomato sauce was almost as thick as the bread part.

The pizza was already cut into wedge-shaped slices. I tried to take a piece, but the melted cheese made it stick to its neighbors. When I finally pulled it free, long strings of cheese dangled down and whipped about.

One strand flapped into Debbie's face. She

shrieked. I was afraid it had burned her, but fortunately she was only startled.

The others didn't seem to have any trouble, though. They must have had a lot of practice. I watched carefully to see how they managed the cheese, but I still wished I had a pair of chopsticks to pick up the strands.

"How did you celebrate birthdays in China, Mary?" asked Kim.

"We ate noodles — you know, chow mein," I said. "Noodles are long, so they stand for a long life."

"That's weird," said Debbie. "I can't imagine eating noodles for birthdays."

"Do you always eat pizza for birthdays?" I asked.

"Mary's got you there, Debbie," said Kim. "You know, pizza is originally from Italy, and hot dogs are from Germany. Now they're both American!" Kim rolled her eyes, and the others laughed.

We were just finishing when Jason came in the door. He had been at soccer practice, but now he had come back to drive us all to the movie theater.

Jason said proudly that he had turned sixteen a few weeks ago and the first thing he'd done was to get his driver's license. I wasn't thrilled to be driven by someone who had just got his license, but nobody else seemed worried.

As we drove, Jill asked Holly about her viola lessons. "Are you going to try out for the Junior Chamber Orchestra?"

"My mom wants me to," said Holly. "My teacher is having me play a sonata by Brahms. I hope the accompanist can have it practiced by next week. It's a really hard piece."

"I'm sure you'll get in to the orchestra," said Jill.

"Jason, you play the piano, don't you?" asked Debbie.

Jason shook his head. "Nah, I've got better things to do these days. Soccer takes up most of my time."

I was shocked to hear that playing soccer was a better thing to do than playing the piano. "You really think sports are more important than music?" I asked Jason. Although I had begged Eldest Brother to take up a sport, I wouldn't dream of asking him to *give up* music for athletics.

Jason just shrugged. "Sure, and most guys would agree." He laughed. "Jeez, if I told the coach I had to skip a game to play the piano, everybody would think I was a geek!"

I felt my face burn with anger. A geek was probably what Jason thought Eldest Brother was. "You're just scared, aren't you?" I said to Jason. "You're scared of what the other boys think."

There was a sudden silence. I saw that I had been rude, but it was too late to take back my words. Holly would think this was just another Yang family member not knowing how to behave.

The silence was broken by Kim. "I think Mary is right. We shouldn't give up something we care about just because of what others think."

To my surprise, Jason turned to me and winked. "I wasn't giving up anything I cared about, and the world didn't exactly lose a great concert pianist when I quit."

Jason really didn't seem to mind, and for the rest of the ride, he chatted with the others about his soccer team.

The movie we saw was about a horse that got separated from its owner, a teenage girl. Again, Holly was the one who had chosen the movie, because it was about animals. The others simply went along with her choice. It finally occurred to me that she got her way because she knew her own mind and didn't let others interfere. She was going to be a veterinarian and work with animals, and nothing was going to stop her.

When we came out of the theater, Holly said the movie was one of the most touching she had ever seen. All the others agreed.

"I must have used up a whole packet of Kleenex," said Jill.

"Me, too," said Debbie, sniffing. She turned to me. "Did you like the movie, Mary?"

"Yes, I enjoyed it," I said. And then I surprised myself by saying, "I didn't find it terribly sad, though."

Holly stared at me. "Don't you like horses?"

"Well, I've never seen a live horse in my life," I admitted. "To me it's just an animal — like a deer or a bear. I don't cry over a bear, so why should I care so much about a horse?"

Everybody stared. Apparently I had said something shocking. "I care a lot about kittens, though," I added quickly.

Holly was still frowning, and the other girls looked away from me. I was in disgrace. We stood around without saying anything until Jason drove by to pick us up.

In the car I tried hard to think of a way to get

back Holly's approval, but there wasn't enough time since I was the first one to be dropped off. It was just my luck that Second Sister opened the front door as Jason pulled up to our house.

There was no help for it. Everyone in the car saw Second Sister in her full Chinese costume. She had on her short jacket with the high collar, and her wrist stuck out three inches because she had grown since coming to America. She was also wearing her cloth shoes, the ones with holes.

As I walked away from the car, I heard a giggle from Debbie. "Boy, Mary's sister sure likes to show she's different, doesn't she?"

I wanted to die.

Then I heard Kim's voice. "You know, that's what I like about Mary's family: They don't care what people think about them."

Maybe the rest of the Yangs didn't care, but I did.

9

I tried to squeeze my left leg behind my cello case in the backseat. It was a week after Kim's birthday party, and we were on the way to a rehearsal of the All-City Orchestra. The best players from the Seattle elementary schools had been selected to form a citywide orchestra, which rehearsed once a week.

Holly and I had been chosen from our school; so had Kim. The rehearsals were held in an auditorium across town from our neighborhood, so Mrs. Hanson and Mrs. O'Meara took turns driving the three of us to the rehearsals.

It was nice of Mrs. Hanson and Mrs. O'Meara to include me. My cello was only half-size, but it still took up a lot of room, and I had a struggle fitting it in the car.

"What time is your tryout on Wednesday,

Holly?" asked Mrs. Hanson, who was driving that week. "I have to make sure I can get time off to take you over."

Holly was silent for a moment. "I might have to call it off. The accompanist is sick, and I'm not sure she'll be able to play."

Mrs. Hanson turned her head sharply to look at Holly. The car swerved, and she got it back into the lane before she spoke again. "But that's awful! You've been practicing the piece for ages! And it's too late for you to prepare some unaccompanied piece! Why didn't you tell me earlier?"

"It's not the end of the world, Mom," muttered Holly.

"Can't your music teacher find another accompanist?" asked Mrs. Hanson. "There must be other pianists around!"

"It's a hard piece, that Brahms. We won't be able to get anybody ready by Wednesday."

I could see the tendons on Mrs. Hanson's neck. It occurred to me that *she* was the one who was really bothered, not Holly.

A brilliant idea suddenly hit me. "Mrs. Hanson, my mother can play the accompaniment for Holly's tryout."

We had arrived at the auditorium. Mrs. Hanson stopped the car and slowly turned to look at me. "Are you sure? She can't stop if she makes a mistake, you know. It would ruin Holly's piece."

Mother might do a lot of embarrassing things, but if there was one thing I felt confident about, it was her musical ability. "My mother has played a lot of chamber music with other people, so she never loses the beat even if she makes a mistake."

"Thank you for the offer, Mary," Mrs. Hanson said. But she still looked doubtful.

It might be mean of me, but I hoped Holly's accompanist would stay sick. This was a chance for Mother to get on Mrs. Hanson's good side for a change. Holly would be grateful to me for saving her audition, and she might forget what I had said about horses.

Halfway through the rehearsal we had a break. Holly came to the cello section and made her way to my stand. "Can I talk to you for a minute, Mary?"

I could tell that she was unhappy about something. "Sure, Holly," I said. "What's wrong?"

She absently ran her finger across the horsehair of her viola bow, and some of the resin flew up in a fine powder. "It's about your mother accompanying me for the tryout," she said finally. "I don't really care about getting in to the Junior Chamber Orchestra, you know. My mom wants me to join, because it's such a select group and they have a summer camp on Orcas Island."

A summer camp where people just made music! It sounded like heaven. Playing in the All-City Orchestra was fun, but being in the Junior Chamber Orchestra would be a real privilege. I tried not to feel envious. "I'd give anything to join something like that! Is it very expensive?"

Holly nodded. "It costs a bundle, but my dad will pay for it. In fact he's one of the main supporters of the orchestra. But frankly, I'd rather have the money for something else — like raising purebred dogs."

She grimaced as she looked around the rehearsal hall. I didn't know what to say. Were we really that different? Did she really think purebred dogs are more important than music?

On the way home, Mrs. Hanson seemed more friendly. "Your mother is a professional pianist, isn't she? Maybe I *will* ask her to play for Holly's tryout if the regular accompanist can't make it, Mary."

I looked at Holly and saw that she was gently

shaking her head. If I asked Mother to play the accompaniment, Holly might get mad and wouldn't let me be her friend anymore. After I had worked so hard to get this far with her!

Then I thought of Mother. I thought of how many social blunders she had been making. If she got to play in Holly's tryout, the Hansons would find out what a good pianist she was and respect her a lot more.

It was hard to decide. So I just mumbled something.

"Fine!" Mrs. Hanson said cheerfully. "I'll give your mother a call tomorrow."

As Mrs. Hanson dropped me at our house, I ran into Mr. and Mrs. Sylvester. "We saw that kitten again, Mary," said Mr. Sylvester. "It seems to hang around a lot. I wonder if it's a stray. Maybe we can take it home."

"I don't want a cat, Benny," said Mrs. Sylvester. "Cats are stuck-up animals, and they care only about themselves. I want another dog. I want a beagle like Jenny!"

Her voice quavered a little, and I knew she still missed their dog.

"Now, now, Denny," said Mr. Sylvester. "We'll find a beagle just like Benny one of these days."

When I went in the house, Fourth Brother was making himself a peanut butter and jelly sandwich in the kitchen.

"I thought you didn't like peanut butter," I said.

"I knew you were embarrassed because I was always eating bean sprouts for lunch," he said. "So I thought I'd try to get used to peanut butter."

It was nice that Fourth Brother cared about my feelings. He took a big bite of the sandwich. "Anyway, I couldn't find anything else to eat," he mumbled.

I remembered why I wanted to talk to him. "Did you hear what the Sylvesters said? They saw Rita again!"

Fourth Brother licked the peanut butter from the roof of his mouth and swallowed. Then he said, "It's okay as long as she comes when I play the dinner signal."

"But if Mrs. Sylvester gets another dog, it might tear Rita to pieces!"

"We'll have to talk her out of it," said Fourth Brother.

That was easy enough to say. But what could we do if the Sylvesters finally found a beagle to replace Jenny?

I had too many things to worry about. Rita kept escaping from the basement. Having Mother accompany Holly might ruin my friendship with her. And my family kept disgracing themselves in public.

Once I saw a juggling act in China. A girl balanced three plates simultaneously by spinning them at the ends of three chopsticks. I felt like that juggler. At any minute, one of the plates might fall and smash into bits.

Mrs. Hanson called Tuesday night when we were having dinner. I answered the phone. "Mary," she said, "do you still think your mother could play the accompaniment tomorrow for Holly's audition?"

I felt torn. If I said yes, I risked losing Holly's friendship. But if she didn't want to be in the orchestra, why couldn't she just play badly at the audition? Maybe she was too proud. She didn't want her mother to see that she wasn't good enough or that she wasn't trying hard.

From where I stood in the hallway, I could see into the dining room. Mother was bringing in a stir-fried dish, and after setting it down, she wiped her forehead.

"I know it's very short notice," Mrs. Hanson was saying. "Hello? Are you still there, Mary?"

I cleared my throat. "Yes, Mrs. Hanson. I'm sure my mother would be able to do it. Can you bring the music over tonight?"

Mrs. Hanson breathed a sigh of relief. "Thank you, Mary. I'll be over as soon as I can."

"Well, we're still having supper. . . ," I told her.

"Of course, of course!" she said quickly. "I'll come at eight, shall I?"

It was strange to hear Mrs. Hanson sounding so anxious to please. I told her that eight o'clock was fine, then walked slowly back to the dining-room table.

The family looked at me curiously. "What was that about?" asked Father.

"Mother," I said in a rush, "Mrs. Hanson needs a pianist to play the accompaniment for Holly's tryout. It's a Brahms viola sonata. She's bringing over the music tonight at eight. Can you do it?"

Mother's face turned pink. I could tell she was pleased. "Why, yes, I think I can. Is that the one transposed from a violin sonata?"

I didn't know, but Father and Eldest Brother

did. For the rest of the meal, we discussed the piece and whether Mother could play it at such short notice.

Mother wasn't the only one who looked happy. Father said it was about time people learned how good Mother was, while Eldest Brother and Second Sister both beamed and nodded agreement.

Fourth Brother was the only one who didn't look completely happy. "I hope Mrs. Hanson doesn't mention Rita," he said to me as the two of us cleared the table.

I had forgotten about Rita! Mrs. Hanson was under the impression that we had already told my family about her. I had to prevent Mrs. Hanson from saying something.

Mrs. Hanson and Holly arrived promptly at eight. Mrs. Hanson looked around at our living room. I had given up trying to neaten the room, and there were music stands all over. My cello leaned against the sofa, and next to it was an open case containing Elder Brother's violin. Heaps of sheet music were piled on the stands, on the sofa, and on the floor. To walk across the room, you had to negotiate carefully between piles.

"Goodness, you have a lot of music!" Mrs. Hanson exclaimed. "If you had the kitten in here . . ."

I knew what she was going to say next, and I had to head her off. Before I could do anything, there was a clatter behind me. Fourth Brother had acted first: He had knocked over a couple of music stands.

As I helped him set the stands up again, he whispered to me, "You'll have to think of something else to distract her."

"As I was saying —," Mrs. Hanson began again.

"Mother," I interrupted desperately, "we haven't tuned the piano for some time. Do you think that will bother Holly?"

Mother walked over to the piano and played a blurringly fast chromatic scale across the keyboard. "It should do well enough." She turned to Mrs. Hanson. "Have you got the music?"

At last that took Mrs. Hanson's mind from Rita — for the time being. She fetched the music and handed it to Mother.

Mother looked at the score. "My husband thought it might be this sonata. I've accompanied him on it — in a different key, of course." She sat down at the piano and looked at Holly. "Shall we try it?"

Holly looked uncomfortable — the first time I had ever seen her really uncomfortable. Slowly, she took out her viola and tuned it. "I'm getting stage fright," she muttered, looking around at the circle of eyes.

"Then it would be good practice for the real audition," said Mrs. Hanson with a nervous laugh.

We moved aside piles of instruments and music and found seats. Holly and Mother began.

After a few bars, I began to worry — but not about Mother. There was nothing wrong with her piano playing. She had played the piece before, after all.

The problem was Holly. She had obviously been well taught. Her bowing was correct, her fingering neat, and her pitch true. She seemed to be following the score carefully, obeying all the dynamics signs. But there was something lifeless about her playing — and that was fatal.

My family and I looked around at one another, and I saw the same conclusion in everybody's eyes. Even Fourth Brother, who can't tell "Old MacDonald Had a Farm" from "Mary Had a

Little Lamb," seemed to know from the expression on Holly's face that her heart wasn't in the music.

At the end we all clapped politely, but nobody was fooled. "I told you I had stage fright," Holly said in a low voice.

Mrs. Hanson swallowed. "You'll get over it by tomorrow, darling," she said, and the forced smile on her face was painful to see. She turned to Mother. "Thank you very much, Mrs. Yang. You played beautifully."

"Oh, no, I was simply awful!" said Mother. She knew she had done well, but for a Chinese it would be very rude to agree.

"You're a marvelous pianist, really!" insisted Mrs. Hanson.

Mother again disagreed. "I'm very poor. You must not flatter me."

"No, no!" said Mrs. Hanson. "I'm not trying to flatter you."

Holly looked impatient. "Mom, we'd better go."

"Of course, darling," Mrs. Hanson said quickly. She turned to Mother. "Holly has to get a good night's rest. We don't want her to go to the audition all tired and sleepy, do we?"

"Yes!" said Mother, smiling broadly.

Mrs. Hanson blinked. "I mean, we wouldn't want Holly to fail the audition!"

"Yes, yes!" said Mother.

The rest of the Yangs agreed. "Yes," we all said earnestly.

Mrs. Hanson and Holly stared at us. I could tell that something was wrong, but I didn't know what it was. Finally Mrs. Hanson turned abruptly and walked to the front door. "Good night!" she said curtly. Opening the door, she walked out, followed by Holly.

I went after them, determined to find out what the matter was.

"Uh — did my mother say something funny again just now?" I asked when I had caught up with the Hansons.

Mrs. Hanson stopped. "Well, it just sounded awfully strange, what all of you said. I could hardly believe my ears!"

I didn't know what she was talking about. "What did we say? What sounded strange?"

"It sounded like you wanted me to fail the audition!" said Holly.

It was my turn not to believe my ears. "We said no such thing!"

"I said we wouldn't want Holly to fail the audition," Mrs. Hanson said slowly, very slowly. "Then your family said yes — every single one of you!"

"Of course we said yes!" I cried indignantly. "We agreed with you completely! We certainly don't want Holly to fail the audition!"

The three of us stood frozen and looked at one another. To a passerby, we must have looked like three store dummies.

Suddenly Mrs. Hanson began to laugh. "Yes! We have no bananas!" she sang in a high, cracked voice.

She had gone completely mad! Maybe the anxiety over Holly's audition had driven her out of her mind. I looked at Holly. But she was laughing as well. "It's an old song my grandma used to sing," she told me.

Mrs. Hanson turned to me, still laughing. "You all said yes because you agreed with me, just like in the song 'Yes! We Have No Bananas.' "

I still didn't understand. "Was that wrong?"

Holly tried to explain. "In English, you'd say, 'No, we wouldn't want Holly to fail the audition.' "

I had thought that learning English was just a matter of memorizing a lot of new words and phrases. It is much more complicated than that. Even knowing when to say yes or no is tricky!

I turned slowly away and started for home. I'd have a lot to write in my notebook tonight. Behind my back, I heard Mrs. Hanson and Holly giggling and softly singing, "Yes! We have no bananas today!"

Suddenly I felt I had to say something. I turned again and caught up with the Hansons. "Mrs. Hanson," I said, "we're new in this country, and we can't do everything right immediately. I hope you'll try to be patient."

Without waiting for her to reply, I turned to Holly. "When you picked up your viola for the first time, you probably played a few sour notes. I bet your teacher didn't break down laughing."

By now both Mrs. Hanson and Holly had sobered. "You're quite right, Mary," Mrs. Hanson said quietly. "We should have been more understanding."

She looked at Holly. "You should apologize, too."

Holly murmured something. Her face didn't show much expression, so I couldn't tell how she felt.

As I walked home, I thought about how unfair I had been to my family all these months. I thought they had been impossible, because they didn't make more of an effort to learn American ways.

But I am actually one of them: In spite of my list of new words and my careful study of American ways, I still make mistakes, just like the rest of the family.

I had blamed Mother more than the rest, because she had made the most embarrassing mistakes. I should have remembered that she had to spend all her time cooking and feeding us. She didn't have time to meet a lot of Americans and learn the customs of this country.

I had been ashamed of Mother. Now I was more ashamed of myself.

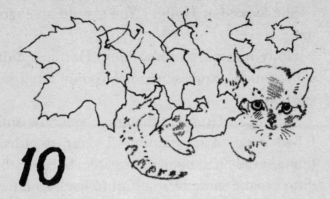

10

I was hovering near the front door when Mrs. Hanson dropped Mother off after Holly's audition. Neither Mrs. Hanson nor Holly came into the house, and that gave me some idea of how the audition had gone.

I followed Mother into the kitchen, where she began to wash greens for dinner. "Did Holly play well?" I asked.

Mother sighed. "She didn't make any mistakes, but . . ."

She didn't have to say any more. Holly probably hadn't put much feeling into her playing, and the judges must have known right away.

By offering my mother as a replacement, I had forced Holly to play at the tryout. Now, if she failed to get into the orchestra, she would probably be angry at me.

The next day at school, I wanted to ask Holly about the audition, but she always seemed to be busy talking to one of the girls in her group, and I never got a chance to speak to her alone. Could she be avoiding me? That was a bad sign.

We had an All-City rehearsal after school, and it was Mrs. O'Meara's turn to drive. She was busy, so Jason took us.

During the break in the rehearsal, I made my way over to Holly in the viola section, but she was busy talking to her stand partner about the piece we were rehearsing. Since she almost never discussed music, I suspected she was deliberately avoiding me.

On the way back, Jason drove to my house first as usual. I knew that something was wrong even before he stopped the car. Fourth Brother was standing by the curb, obviously waiting for me. Mr. Sylvester was under the big maple tree in our yard, looking up into the branches.

I jumped out of the car and looked up. Rita was sitting on a branch high above the ground, mewing in a thin, pitiful voice.

"What happened?" I whispered to Fourth Brother.

He shrugged. "I don't know. When I got home from school, I saw Mr. Sylvester in the yard. Rita was already up in the tree by then."

Mr. Sylvester turned around. "Oh, there you are, Mary. See, there's that stray kitten I was telling you about. I'm sure it's homeless."

"How did it get in the tree?" I asked.

"I was just petting it, and it was purring like an engine," said Mr. Sylvester. "Then some idiot with a dog came down the street. The dog barked and scared the kitten into the tree."

Kim opened her mouth, but I spoke first. "How long has it been up there?"

"Since this morning," said Mr. Sylvester. "I tried to reach it, but it just climbed higher."

Mrs. Sylvester came out. "What are we going to do, Denny? You want to call the fire department?"

Mr. Sylvester hesitated. "If they come and rescue the kitten, they might send it to the pound."

"Maybe somebody can climb up," suggested Kim. She turned around. "Jason, do you think you can reach the kitten?"

Jason came slowly out of the car and looked up. "Gee, I don't know — it's awfully high up."

"Jason O'Meara," demanded Kim, "are you scared to climb up the tree?"

Jason looked away. "I'm allergic to cats. You know that, Kim."

Rita mewed again, but she sounded fainter. Was it my imagination, or was she getting weaker? She seemed to be draped limply over the tree branch.

"It's a long way to the ground," I said nervously.

Fourth Brother seemed to think the same thing. "She could hurt herself if she fell!"

Mr. Sylvester patted his shoulder. "Don't worry, kid. I've heard cats can fall off a four-story building and turn around just in time to land safely on their feet."

"Cats can do that only if they are fully conscious," said Holly. She had gotten out, too, and was looking up anxiously at Rita. "But Rit — uh — this kitten looks faint."

Even Mr. Sylvester looked concerned. "Yeah, maybe we'd better call the fire department after all. What do you think, Denny?"

Mother and Second Sister came out of the house. "What's all the commotion?" asked Mother.

Second Sister saw us pointing and glanced up at the tree. "Mother, look at that little kitten stuck up there!" She began to mew in a high voice and crooned, "Come on, come on down."

Rita raised her head and looked down when she heard the mewing but made no move to jump.

"Poor thing," said Mother. "Maybe I can tempt it to back down with a bit of food."

She hurried into the house and came back with a dish of leftovers. "Here, kitty! Here's a treat for you!" she called.

Again Rita's ears flickered. She gathered herself together, and for a moment I really thought she was going to jump. But she slumped back. The height still scared her.

Father joined us at the foot of the tree. "I'll see if I can find a rather," he said.

Father had meant to say "ladder." He knew that he had trouble with *r* and *th*, and for days, he had been hard at work practicing and muttering, "Rice, river, with, wither . . ." But now he'd gone and overdone things. Fortunately everyone else was too preoccupied to notice.

All Father could find was a stepladder, which fell far short of Rita's tree limb.

I looked around at my family, and I felt a rush of love for them. Even if they weren't successful, they were all doing their best to help Rita.

They didn't just stand around looking horrified.

"What's happening?" asked Eldest Brother as he came out of the house, still holding his violin. "I can't concentrate, with all this noise."

"He can't concentrate," mimicked Jason, speaking in a wimpy voice. I wanted to kick him.

Eldest Brother ignored him. He joined the rest of us at the foot of the tree and looked up. "So it *was* a kitten after all! I *thought* I was hearing a kitten, but everybody kept telling me it was a squeaky door!"

"Can you do something, Eldest Brother?" I asked.

Eldest Brother peered at the branches of the tree, especially at the one closest to the ground. "Hmm . . . yes, I think I can get up there." He handed his violin to Fourth Brother.

"Are you going to climb up to the kitten?" asked Mother. "It's awfully high up."

"She might scratch your eyes when you reach her," warned Holly.

Eldest Brother shook his head. "It won't scratch my eyes if I put it in a bag. Remember when I used to climb up persimmon trees in China, Third Sister?"

I remembered. When I was smaller, the persimmon trees looked tremendously tall, and I was filled with awe at the way Eldest Brother climbed higher than any of the other boys and got the ripe fruit nobody else could reach. He would take a bag up with him, put the fruit in the bag, and stuff it down his shirt. He could bring us a whole bag of ripe persimmons, almost bursting with sweet juice.

"I'll get a paper bag," I said, running into the house.

When I went back to the tree with the bag, more people had gathered in the yard. Besides our family, the Sylvesters, Holly, Kim, and Jason, there were neighbors from down the street. I heard murmurs as they discussed whether it was safe for Eldest Brother to climb up to Rita.

The crowd fell silent as Eldest Brother

jumped up and reached the lowest branch. He
swung himself up until he sat on top of the
branch. He looked up at the next branch, the
one just below Rita.

I was nervous. It was a long way between his
branch and Rita's. Eldest Brother reached out

for it, and with a mighty heave, swung himself up. I breathed a deep sigh.

Beside me, Jason whistled. "Not bad."

"Your brother is stronger than he looks, Mary," said Kim.

Even Holly seemed impressed. I was nearly exploding with pride. "All that practicing develops strong arm muscles," I told the others.

What happened next made us all gasp with dismay. Rita, nervous at the approach of a stranger just below her, started to retreat toward the tip of her branch. In a moment she would be out of reach!

Quickly Fourth Brother put his violin under his chin and drew the bow across the strings. *Di-di-di-dah, screech!*

I saw Rita's ears flick. She stopped retreating and looked at the ground. Was she going to jump down? But it was too far!

Eldest Brother grabbed.

The next few moments were confusing. Down on the ground we gasped and screamed. Up in the tree Rita hissed with outrage and Eldest Brother yelled with pain. I closed my eyes, unable to look. Then I heard the rustling of the paper bag.

When I opened my eyes and looked up, Eldest Brother's face was scratched but it had a wide grin. The front of his shirt bulged and heaved. The Yangs yelled in Chinese, *"Hao! Hao!"* while the others cried, "Nice going!" or "Wow!"

When Eldest Brother reached the ground safely, he handed the tattered, writhing paper bag to me with relief. "Persimmons never scratched like this!" he said.

Rita struggled out of the bag and jumped to the ground. She looked around eagerly. She had heard the dinner music, and she expected food.

"I'll get some milk," said Fourth Brother, heading for the house.

Everybody had seen Rita now. There was no way we could hide her anymore. Desperately, I tried to think of a way to explain her to my family.

11

Frantically, I looked over to Holly for help. But she said nothing. It was Kim who jumped to my rescue. "Poor little kitten!" she crooned. "She looks lost. Maybe I can take her home with me."

Jason whirled around. "What are you talking about, Kim? You know I'm allergic to cats!"

He turned to Eldest Brother. "I couldn't go up for the kitten because of my allergy. But you did okay."

He opened the door of the car. "Well, I have to get home. Mom needs the car. Coming, Kim?"

Kim shook her head. "Later. I can walk home."

Jason looked almost shy as he waved good-bye to us. I didn't think he would call Eldest

Brother a wimp again.

After Jason left, Mr. Sylvester cleared his throat. "I'd like to adopt the kitten, if it really doesn't belong to anyone."

"But Denny," protested Mrs. Sylvester, "I thought we were going to get another beagle!"

Mr. Sylvester picked up Rita. She purred, and he smiled foolishly. "We can name her Jenny if you want."

Mrs. Sylvester stroked Rita, and her face softened. "Well, if you're set on it. But promise me that if the kitten's owner shows up, we'll get a dog."

Fourth Brother and I, the kitten's owners, looked at each other. We looked at Holly. Almost as one, the three of us nodded in agreement. It was as good a solution as we could expect. Rita would be able to get out of the dark basement and live with the Sylvesters, and I would be able to play with her occasionally. Still, I felt a pang at the thought of losing her.

With a sigh of relief, Fourth Brother handed the violin back to Eldest Brother.

Eldest Brother took the instrument. "I'd better wash my scratches and go back to my practicing."

Kim looked at him as he left. "Your brother

didn't care when Jason called him a wimp. Now that everyone thinks he's a hero for climbing the tree, he just wants to go back to his practicing."

Finally, I realized it *is* possible to be different and still get respect from people. Since arriving in this country, I had been frantically studying American customs and trying to make myself into a native. Well, I would continue to keep my lists of new English words and learn American customs. But that didn't mean I had to be ashamed of my family all the time and change their ways.

If Kim respected them in spite of their differences, I should respect them, too. Most of all, I should respect *myself*.

Mother invited Holly and Kim into the house for a snack. As we sat around the kitchen munching almond cookies, Mother asked the question I hadn't been able to ask. "Did you get into the Junior Chamber Orchestra, Holly?"

Holly shook her head. "No, I didn't."

"Aw, gee, Holly, after all your hard work!" said Kim. "Your mom must be feeling awfully disappointed, too."

"Don't worry, she'll live," Holly said shortly. She got up and went to the door. "I have to run. Thanks for the snack, Mrs. Yang."

It was hard to tell how she felt — if she felt anything at all.

Kim and I looked at each other after Holly had left. "Holly told me she didn't really want to join the orchestra," I said finally. "She's probably not that upset."

"But her dad was at the tryout," said Kim. "He's a big supporter of the orchestra, so he must be really disappointed!"

"You know what?" I said. "I don't think Holly cares how her parents feel."

"I'd feel really lousy if I let my parents down like that!" said Kim.

"Things that would bother us don't matter to Holly," I said.

Kim glanced at me. "You feel that way, too?"

I nodded. "The other night I got mad and yelled at her for laughing at our mistakes in English. I thought she'd be offended, but she didn't care at all."

Suddenly I had a strange feeling. It was like mornings when Mother came into my room to wake me up: The door would open, and a stir of cool air would wake me. I would open my eyes to the real world, while my dreams gradually faded away.

"I don't think I'll ever be real friends with

Holly," I said softly. "We're much too different."

My family might do things that embarrassed me, but I would be deeply upset if I saw them really hurt. To Holly, her parents' feelings truly didn't matter. All that counted was achieving her own goal.

I looked at Kim. If she was jealous of my friendship with Holly, she would be delighted at what I'd said. But she didn't seem glad at all. "You know something, Mary?" she said slowly. "Ever since kindergarten, I always thought I was Holly's best friend. Now I'm beginning to think I was wrong all these years. She lives in her own world, and she doesn't let other people in."

"Maybe she cares more about animals than people," I said.

I had worked so hard to catch Holly's attention. I had done things not because I wanted to but because I thought they'd please her. It was all a wasted effort.

I should have felt devastated. For months, it had been my dearest wish to become Holly's special friend, and now I knew that would never happen.

But strange to say, I wasn't broken-hearted. I felt relieved.

*   *   *

These days I still eat lunch with Holly and her group, but I usually sit next to Kim and talk with her more than with Holly. I can talk to her honestly about things that are on my mind, and I don't have to do any pretending.

My family is still impossible sometimes. I guess they'll always do things that make people laugh. But I no longer break out in a cold sweat when it happens.

Kim said that Jason told all his friends about Rita's rescue, and the boys have stopped calling Eldest Brother a wimp. Fourth Brother's friends still call him Sprout, although he eats peanut butter sandwiches — sometimes.

Kim finally came to our house and played the Mozart flute quartet with us. At first she was so embarrassed by her mistakes that she didn't want to return. Eldest Brother talked her into coming again. Now she plays with us almost every week.

The Sylvesters are delighted with Rita. At first they wanted to call her Denny, but Fourth Brother and I convinced them that it wasn't right to give her a dog's name.

"Why don't you call her Rita?" I said. "After

Rita Hayworth." I just couldn't imagine the kitten — *our* kitten — with any other name.

Mr. Sylvester's eyes brightened. "Rita Hayworth!" he breathed. "I like it! I like it!"

Mrs. Sylvester frowned at him, but he didn't notice.

The other day, Mr. Sylvester complained to us. "Every time your brother plays that *di-di-di-dah* and screech on his d —"

"Now, Denny, watch your language," warned Mrs. Sylvester. "There are youngsters present."

"Anyway, as soon as we hear that tune, the kitten runs off and disappears. Can you explain it?"

Fourth Brother and I looked at each other and smiled.

Whenever we want to play with Rita in our basement, this is the way we get her to come. But we weren't about to tell the Sylvesters. That was *our* secret!

Rita settled down happily in her new home. Like me, she left one home to live in another, just as I left China to live in America. I'm happy in America now and feel I belong here. But a part of me will always remember China.

As Father had said when Second Sister kept playing Chinese folk songs, we shouldn't forget the music of our old home. I think Rita will always remember the music of her old home, even if it's only the screechy dinner tune on Fourth Brother's violin.

di di di da h h h h

SCREECH